The Hive
By Carter Seagrove

Copyright© 2024 The Alderbourne Press Ltd

The Hive

Written by Alp Mortal and Chambers Mars, writing as Carter Seagrove

Edited by Morgan Starr

Cover Design by Alp Mortal

All rights reserved. No part of this publication may be reproduced, distributed or transmitted in any form or by any means, or stored in a database or retrieval system without the prior written permission of the publisher. This book is for your personal enjoyment only. This book may not be re-sold. Thank you for respecting the hard work of this author.

Disclaimer: This is a work of fiction. All of the characters, places and events portrayed in this novel are either products of the author's imagination or are used fictitiously.

Published by

The Alderbourne Press Ltd

Falmouth, Cornwall, UK

2024

Author's Note

Homestead is the last bastion of human civilisation.

Life in *Homestead* is dull, monotonous, and dominated by The Hive – the massive cryogenic facility in which half the population spends half the year, to preserve scant resources.

At sixteen years of age, every young man and woman is paired and told simply -

"You will grow to love each other; you will care for each other; you will produce children together."

Those on the outside serve The Hive, patiently waiting for the one day, every six months, when they are reunited with their partners, albeit briefly, before entering cryo themselves for the next six months. This cycle is all anyone has ever known.

Dull, monotonous, and harsh.

Except, not everyone follows the rules.

David and Peter have a secret – they're in love. Toby has a secret – he mates with anyone pining for their loved one. Management has a secret – a diabolical, immoral, and potential lethal secret. Should anyone find out what it is, all hell will break loose …

Ronan, a maintenance operative and one of the very few that gets to go to the very top of The Hive, sees something beyond the city wall, and it poses a question, challenging the status quo … Are we the lone survivors of the holocaust after all?

A chance discovery by Peter, allied with Ronan's suspicion, sets wheels in motion.

Born into servitude, believing there is nothing beyond the wall, accepting nothing will ever change, insurgence is the furthest thing from anyone's mind until, one day, a line is crossed, and the terrible truth is exposed, with catastrophic and far-reaching consequences for everyone.

It is nothing compared to what they find outside the wall.

The Hive is written by Alp Mortal and Chambers Mars, writing as Carter Seagrove (further titles produced by this collaboration include *Dust Jacket* and *The Inspector Fenchurch Mysteries*).

Also, look out for the accompanying story – Toby's Day.

Chapter One - Open Day

Attuned, as ever, to the slightest change in the hum of the ventilators because that could spell disaster if the supply were ever interrupted, even before the door opened, he'd heard the tell-tale *whoosh* of the outer curtain fall back, and he pushed the book into its makeshift *plasto* sheath and slipped it back into the water cistern, replacing the lid quickly. Turning, just as the door slid open, he had a ready smile waiting for Gwen.

"David!"

"Hello, Gwen-"

"There's just time to get back and change; we have to get the food ready. What's keeping you?"

"I had some trays to clean; I'll be ready in two minutes."

"Hurry up then; we don't want to be stuck at the back!"

Swallowing down a balloon of dread mixed with excitement, which was like an egg in his throat, he swiftly grabbed the two trays from the bench and plunged them into the sink, automatically reaching for the scourer and soap.

"Manager wouldn't mind if you left those, you know; not today of all days!"

"Relax, Gwen; there's plenty of time ..."

She busied herself by grabbing a stack of *plastoboard* tubes, expertly folding the ends to make a dozen little containers, which she placed in the rack with the others. It was one of those jobs that you just did without thinking, like returning the trays to the drying frame or checking in on the latest batch of the *spiro* - as it was most often called - to see that it was drying evenly and not crisping at the edges.

"... I don't want to leave anything left undone before *bye-byes*."

"Peter will appreciate it ... Marion doesn't usually care two hoots about anything."

He could never understand why he didn't feel even the slightest bit irked that Gwen held such a low opinion of his partner. Mention of her partner's name brought the same rosy blush to his cheeks as it always did.

"Marion cares but in other ways ..."

He couldn't think of any offhand, but it felt right to come to her defence.

"Hurry up!"

"I'm done, woman! Go and turn the lights out while I dry my hands ..."

Gwen scuttled off to the control bank and flipped the switches, leaving the room bathed in just the pale, phosphorous green of the security downlighters. The whirr of the oxygen harvesters lessened a few decibels.

They left the farm and entered the short tunnel that led to the inner compound. Gwen inched ahead, keen to get outside and enjoy the last few hours of fresh air and light.

David felt his feet grow heavier and heavier with each step.

Passing out through the heavy *plasto* curtain into the courtyard, they met Manager, who was locking up the office.

"Come on, you two!"

Gwen doubled her pace to catch him up, urging David to, "Hurry up!"

As they passed over the dike that surrounded the farm, the sounds of the inhabitants of *Homestead* reached their ears - excited shouts, the laughter of dozens of children, and the unmistakable screech of the brood mothers, sitting on their precious clutches of eggs.

The sense of anticipation and excitement was palpable.

Following the roadway, which was flanked on both sides by the huge ductwork that ferried the oxygen from the farm to the Hive, they overtook the last few members of the cleaner gang on duty as they swept the dust from the top of the duct housing, capturing the debris in the mobile vacuum unit.

"Why do the cleaners never join us at the feast, Manager?"

"You know why, Gwen ..."

"Yes; I know they have fewer rights than us ... but why?"

Like so much in *Homestead*, it was a given; cleaners had no rights, they did not join the feast, and they never went into *cryo*.

"Continuity, Gwen ... there has to be *continuity*."

David listened, wishing *he* was a cleaner, scanning the backs of the men who were sweeping up, tormented by the idea of wearing just shorts, feeling the sweat running down his back, and the scorching midday sun burning his forearms and turning his hair pale gold. These ideas were nothing to the visions he had of sharing a bunk room, showering together, and fucking mindlessly - if the rumours could be believed.

"Do you have a name yet, David?" Manager asked.

Dragging his attention back to his companions, he replied, "Sorry?"

"A name for the baby; do you have a name for the baby?"

"Oh; Marion wanted *Charlotte* if it was a girl."

"And if it's a boy?"

"*Camden* ..."

"I know we should not hope but let's wish it is a girl."

Manager, catching David's eye and the tell-tale strain etched into the wrinkles around the eyes and in the set of the jaw, chided her, "We should not *wish*, Gwen ... In any event, you will have your own in due course. A healthy child, whether boy or girl, is a gift to *Homestead*."

Manager threw a smile in David's direction, hoping to levitate the man's mood.

David, in a voice that was barely audible above the hum of the vacuum pump, replied, "A child is a precious gift; we are blessed."

The words felt like grit in his mouth, and his voice sounded dead in his own ears. And just like the gloop he ate every day, the taste of this *gift* made him feel sick, and only a hastily taken glug of *cha* from his flask prevented him from throwing up.

Between the dike and the remnants of the old city walls, they passed through the garlic beds, which ignited their appetites, and the thought of the feast carried them through the gate and into the labyrinth of streets that formed *Dome Town* and their dwellings.

As they turned into the street that was home to the farmers, a huge sigh went up, signalling that the Hive had been opened. It also signalled that an hour alone remained before the time when couples would be reunited for the first time in six months.

oOo

The temporary sanctuary of his dwelling allowed him to take a deep breath.

He barely had time to shower and change his clothes. Fortunately, he'd remembered to strip the bed that morning and exchange the dirty laundry for clean linen at Stores before his shift had commenced.

He took a shower, dried himself, donned his clean clothes, made the bed, and bundled up his dirty uniform and the skanky towel for dropping off on his way to the Hive. Marion would have nothing to do for the first day after emerging from *cryo* except to feed herself. The larder was stacked with crackers and G.L.O.P - everyone said *gloop,* and no one could remember what the letters stood for anymore. Stores would issue her with supplements and, in time, formula for the baby. Her milk would be given over to Stores for processing just as all mothers' milk was. No baby was breastfed.

He thought it was a cruel practice - like so many others. Even Manager's explanation that breastfeeding created a bond too strong to survive the separation of *cryo* did not appease him.

"*Babies should be fed by their mothers, and mothers should not have to be separated from their babies ...*"

He had to wonder at the strength of his feelings given that he felt no real love for Marion.

They had been assigned to each other when they had reached the age of fourteen.

No choice.

No prospect of it ever changing unless one of them died.

"You will grow to love each other; you will care for each other; you will produce children together."

The only instructions that were given at the time.

Their union only officially signified by their matching yellow wrist bands, bearing the same number - *1002*. Except, his was prefixed *M* and hers was prefixed *W*.

The band irritated his wrist. He found himself absently scratching at the same spot.

"David!"

Gwen's call made him start. He took one look around the dwelling and said goodbye.

"Coming!"

He found her outside, fidgeting.

"Why are you dawdling? Don't you want to see Marion? I can't wait to see Peter ..."

She pulled at his sleeve, and he rolled his eyes.

"... We only get four hours! C'mon!!"

"You have a permit; Marion will be whisked off to the clinic."

"Even more reason to make the most of the time you have. I *really* hope I get pregnant this time."

"You will ..."

Marion had been so happy last time. As he'd found her face in the crowd as he'd stepped through into the reception after being processed, she'd waved the slip. It meant she was pregnant; their coupling on the last changeover had been successful.

Once Marion had entered *cryo*, her pod was designated as 'inseminated'. He'd seen the sign every day when he had gone to clean the pod and monitor her vitals. And every day, he had wished they had failed to conceive.

Her six months in the pod had been monitored very closely to ensure that her pregnancy was progressing successfully albeit much more slowly. When he emerged from his imminent six months in *cryo*, he would be welcomed by a baby daughter or son.

Once they'd dropped off their laundry, they moved through Dome Town's outer precinct and into the enclosure. The vast *synthoplex*-clad Hive always took everyone's breath away.

As he and Gwen entered the mess hall, he chided himself for being so miserable. He could have been born a sewer dredger. He was a farmer, which earned him status and respect. He had study time allocated to him. And for the next six months, instead of listening to Gwen's constant chatter about babies, he could dream about the only thing that ever put a smile on his face ...

oOo

'Will all yellow and green bands please report to the lecture hall.'

The announcement had been the most highly anticipated event of the last week. It also coincided the group's birthday - sixteen and no longer classed as children. The call signalled the first time that each pair would be separated, one half spending the next six months in *cryo* while the other half took up their new roles alongside the adults.

Despite having been paired at the age of fourteen, girls and boys spent most of their time in their respective gender-assigned study clubs. After today, each pair would be assigned a dwelling, and the responsibility to care for their partner while they were frozen, which generally meant, cleaning the outside of the pod, and monitoring the flow of oxygen and nutrients, tabulating the results, and reporting weekly to Control.

"Peter! Hurry up!!"

"Wait, David. Why are you so keen to get there? We know what's happening."

"We don't want to miss out on the ice cream."

"I hate ice cream."

"I'll have yours then."

"Where are Gwen and Marion?"

"Where do you think?"

"What is it with girls and dressing their hair?"

"Ask them!"

David waited impatiently as Peter put his books away and slipped his jacket on.

They left the barrack-style study room and headed to the lecture hall, joining the rest of their group, most of whom had been out on defence maintenance, leaving David and Peter to study because both were farmers, and farmers were special, even farmers-in-training.

The jostling and banter were to be expected given the imminent pairing up of young men and women. There was but one thing on everyone's mind as they filed into the lecture hall. The girls used a separate entrance but as soon as they had piled in, everyone found their assigned partner and went to queue for ice cream.

"Do you like my hair?"

Gwen's question, directed at Peter, made Marion's eyes roll. Nevermore grateful for the fact that Marion didn't seem to care as much about what he thought, David grinned as Peter stammered through his reply, turning redder and redder. Only once they found themselves at the head of the queue did Gwen shut up about it.

When everyone was seated, Manager entered the room.

"Pay attention, everyone. Tomorrow, assigned partners will enter the Hive – outside partners will start their care duties before leaving for designated areas. Anyone – ANYONE – who fails to perform their care duties will default. Anyone who misses a designated shift will default – THERE ARE NO EXCUSES!"

Silence as thick as the gloop they ate hung like a blanket, waiting for something - or someone – to do something or say something.

"No questions? Good! Enjoy this time. When you leave here, check the register, and go to your assigned quarters. At nine o'clock tomorrow morning, report at the Hive – anyone who fails to show up will default ... Thank you."

Manager left the room, leaving the hundred couples to contemplate the next fifteen hours. Some commotion at the back of the room grabbed everyone's attention.

"I can't do it!"

Peter was first to his feet, knowing the voice without having to turn.

"Peter! Don't get involved."

"Gwen! It's Ronan, for goodness sake. I can't just stand by and watch him get dragged off!"

Before she could reply – or oblivious to it – he threaded his way through the tables and chairs and just made it to Ronan's side before Medic entered the room with a nurse.

"Ronan!"

"I can't do it, Peter! I just can't-"

But before either of them knew what was happening, the young man had been grabbed and pulled outside, leaving Peter, and Ronan's partner, Amy, agog, unwilling to admit what they both knew would happen.

"Come over to our table, Amy"

"I ... I should have said something. He was acting so strangely this morning – I should have known."

"It'll be okay. C'mon ..."

She allowed him to guide her their table, where Gwen and Marion took charge and bundled her off to the toilet.

"C'mon, Peter; let's go to the farm ..."

"What about the girls?"

"They'll be *forever*. We know what is going to happen to Ronan; there's no point worrying about it."

Escaping, using the commotion in the foyer as camouflage, they quickly checked the register to confirm their dwelling assignment, and hot-footed it to the farm complex, staying in the shadow of the ducting to avoid being spotted by Manager, or worse, Marshal.

Inside the *spiro* room, they found a quiet corner.

"He'll be drugged, and Amy will have to spend the night alone – idiot!" David spat out.

"It could have happened to anyone, David."

"Not us – not after what we said. You still believe it, don't you?"

"Of course – it won't ever change. I promise I'll write everything down."

"I'll look after Gwen; don't worry."

"And I'll look after Marion ... but never forget, it's you I really want."

Before either could think of anything else to say, the outer door banged, and they slipped to the floor to avoid being seen.

"It's the cleaner, Peter ..."

They held their breath.

David felt the pang first – the pang of separation. He reached out and stroked Peter's face gently with his fingertips, moving in behind the gesture to place a kiss on Peter's neck.

A near-inaudible groan escaped Peter's lips, fanning David's cheek with a puff of overly sweet, strawberry-flavoured breath. Before he could move his head away, Peter slipped his hand behind David's neck and pulled him, immediately latching on to his mouth, slipping his tongue between the partly open lips, simultaneously reaching down with his other hand to cup David's balls, kneading them, making him squirm.

"I wanna fuck you, David ..."

"Are you sure?"

"Yes ... Six months is bad enough without the torture of knowing that every day, you'll be just a few feet away."

Without saying a word, he pulled back, turned, and lay flat, bracing himself with one hand, already pushing the back of his trousers down with the other. Over his shoulder, he saw Peter quickly unzip and pull out his cock. His heart skipped a beat. They would have known nothing had they not seen two of the cleaning gang, fucking in the disinfectant store.

On spit alone, Peter lubed up and knelt either side of the toned thighs – the same thighs that had ignited his feelings all those weeks ago when an impromptu storm had forced them to take shelter under the awning beside the sports' equipment store. They were soaked through to the skin. Their thin, *nyleen* shorts provided scant protection from the rain, but ample evidence of the burgeoning need that had not yet found a voice. When Coach had rescued them and provided a warm drink, those furtive glances had melted into a scary but wonderful realisation much like the *choco* flakes that had melted into the milk.

Lowering himself, Peter probed hard, finding access just as easily as his tongue had moments before. Pushing in, he rested his weight on David's back until he was planted. Then, he levered himself up a little to give himself purchase to thrust deeper and swiftly, already overtaken by the feeling to dominate the flesh beneath him. Dominate yet, at the same time, release something, give something, in the same moment, steal everything yet deny nothing.

It made him a little sad that David hadn't again wanted to repay him in-kind. Once he withdrew, milked of his seed, spent and breathless, David quickly finished himself off, avoiding eye contact until his own seed was ejected to a symphony of tacit grimaces.

They cleaned up, giving each other the once over.

A brief but passionate kiss on the lips sealed the bargain.

oOo

"I can't see him!"

"Patience, Gwen; you know the girls come out first ..."

For reasons never fully explained, the younger women came through first, directly into the arms of the young men who had been waiting for them – all had been given slips and ran off to the privilege area. The young men came next, similarly plucked out of the crowd by their girls, to be whisked off without even grabbing any party food first.

The older women were next. An orderly file of women marched out of the processing suite into the reception. The odd cry went up but generally, it was a civilised affair – except for the few who had permits. David found Marion in the column, near the back. She looked pale but still as beautiful as he remembered – golden hair was rare, especially against light skin.

"I see her-"

"Go then – idiot!"

Gwen pushed him forward.

Increasing desperation took hold of him and he quickened his steps. She saw him and raised her hand, smiling wanly. Seconds later, they were reunited for the first time in six months.

"Marion!"

"David!"

He swept her into his arms, pressing his lips to hers, struggling to ignore the deathly pallor to her skin.

"I've fucking missed you!"

"Can we get outside?"

He was taken aback, floored by her haste and refusal to greet Gwen before pulling him towards the doors to the courtyard.

"What's wrong?"

Only when they were as far from the doors as they were allowed to go did she answer.

"I lost the baby ..."

"Oh, Marion ... I'm so sorry. What happened?"

He held her, pressing her close, shushing her tears, which were, in truth, more his than hers, vainly trying to find the right words in response to the broken, choked up sobs.

"They don't know ... I have to have a test ... I can't see Gwen like this; can we go home?"

"Of course ..."

He guided her towards the settlement, cooing softly, secretly hating every fragile molecule he held within his arms, already resigned to missing his reunion with Peter, knowing there would be no chance now.

Once inside their dwelling, he drew off some water for her to drink.

"Do you want anything to eat, Mar'?"

"No, nothing ... thank you. You're missing the party-"

"Don't be silly; I can't leave you."

Before she could reply, there came a rap at the door.

"Who is it?"

"It's Gwen – what's going on?"

David turned toward Marion to ask if she wanted to see her friend.

"Gwen; wait please ... You go, David – don't miss out on everything. We have hours – plenty of time to say goodbye properly."

"Mar-"

"Go! Don't be too long, ok?"

"If you're sure."

"Go ... Bring me back some food, yeah?"

"Ok ..."

He passed Gwen on the threshold.

"Be gentle-"

"Gwen! Come in!"

David strode away, still with tears on his cheeks, but by the time he reached the inner enclosure, his excitement was beginning to hold sway over his genuine sadness at their loss – her loss.

Peter stepped out of the shadow of the water tower just as he started to cross the quadrangle.

"David!"

"Pe-Peter!"

With no thought of the consequences, he threw himself into his lover's arms.

"Thank god!"

The arms that snaked around his torso had never felt so good – like medicine.

"Nurse found Gwen and told her what happened ... I'm so sorry."

"It's hard to understand; I think I'm sad but then I feel relieved – that's wrong, isn't it?"

"I don't know. I'm just so fucking pleased to see you!"

"We don't have much time – where to?"

"Requisitioning? No one will be on duty."

They dived out of sight, running blindly through the alleyways towards Stores.

"You mustn't miss out on your time with Gwen, Peter."

"It's fine – she said to give them an hour ..."

Breathless, they arrived at Stores, and as predicted, no one was on duty. The door was locked.

"Damn!" David cried.

"When did that ever stop us?"

"Where, Peter?"

"Around the back – C'mon!"

Shoehorning themselves in between the edge of the loading bay and the dumpster park, they found a corner – one they had only used in the dim and distant past.

Frantically, they tore at each other, grabbing kisses while ripping their shirts from their backs.

Just as they stepped back to shed their trousers, David placed his hands on Peter's arms, gripping tightly, holding him fast.

"What?"

"I can't keep doing this, Peter – it's too much to bear."

"But ... What choice is there?"

"Escape-"

"Are you out of your fucking mind?"

"I know what they say; we'd survive – I know we would."

"David; don't even *think* it – c'mon or there won't be time."

Reluctantly but with need overtaking any reason or resistance or the compulsion to talk, he turned, bracing himself against the concrete of the bin store retaining wall, thrusting out his buttocks, inviting Peter to invade that space.

With no ceremony, he pressed himself up tight against the hard orbs of his lover's arse and probed, already lightheaded, having to suck in breaths, ignoring the rapidly cooling sweat running down his back.

When his cock was buried to the hilt, only then did he lower himself so that his chest was lying against David's back, and only then did he start to thrust his hips, steadying himself by holding on to David's shoulders, gripping the tight cords of muscle.

"I love you, David ..."

If David replied, he didn't hear it; the blood was rushing through his ears, drowning out everything except the pounding of his heart.

oOo

"We don't have to do anything, David – not this time ..."

Once he had returned to their dwelling, leaving Peter to take a different path when they'd left the farm, finding Marion already in bed, he'd suddenly froze.

"But ... We have to."

"We don't have to do *everything* they say – no one will check, silly. Just lie down ..."

He'd shed his clothes and slipped in under the unnaturally clean sheets – new sheets.

"Just hold me and don't try to think about it. If it happens, all the better. We'll get an automatic pass when I get back – first-timers always do."

"I know ... It's just ... just too cruel to be parted tomorrow."

"Be grateful you're not in Ronan's shoes – I'd hate to be Amy right now – what can she do?"

With a feeling that he began to understand was guilt, he gathered her in his arms and hooked his leg over hers, pressing his soft cock against her thigh.

"Just relax ..."

Her voice was very soothing, he had to admit – he liked her chatter; it quietened the incessant voices that urged him to slide his fingers down over her abdomen and into the tidy little nest of curls that framed the pouty lips that her *nyleen* coverall always hinted at.

She stroked his arm with her free hand, nuzzling into his chest.

"I know we didn't have *any* say in it, but I am very fond of you David – maybe even love you ..."

"I would have chosen you if we had been given a choice."

"Really? I thought you were more interested in Denise ..."

"I like her, but I don't think of her like I think of you."

That seemed to satisfy. He relaxed when he sensed her tension begin to melt away and her breathing become steady.

She shifted, brushing her breast against his side, sending a shiver up his spine, awakening something deep in the pit of his stomach. When he clutched her tighter, she misconstrued the gesture and rolled onto her back, spreading her legs, leaving him with no place to go.

"Make love to me, David ..."

Only by recalling the sight of Peter's glistening cock, and the taste of his sweat, could he begin to get hard. As he slid inside her, it was all he could do not to call out his name.

oOo

"I have to go to Gwen ..."

"I know. I have to see Marion ..."

"It'll go quick – as soon as you close your eyes, you're opening them again – you know how it is."

"I know ... The diary is in the usual place – Please think about-"

"Don't spoil it! It's a fucking stupid idea ... Let's go ..."

They trooped back to Dome Town, grabbing plates of food on their way, ignoring everyone else though most couples had disappeared to their pods for an hour or two. Really only the teens were still out in any numbers.

They parted without a word at the head of the walkway.

Marion was alone.

"Hey! I got you some food ..."

"Thanks. Did you see Peter?"

"Yes, of course ... How are you feeling?"

"Would you believe tired!"

His dry little chuckle was lost in the banging of cups and plates as Marion set the table.

"What did Gwen say?"

"Everything she was expected to say – she's secretly pleased; I know she wanted to get pregnant first-"

"No; she wouldn't wish that!"

"I know her better than you."

He thought that was highly improbable – they spent as much time with her as each other.

"She's just in shock – like we all are."

When it was clear there was nothing further to say, they sat down to eat. The silence was so at odds with the occasion and all previous reunions. Ten years of living this half-life suddenly didn't feel like it had prepared them for anything.

"The new *spiro* is showing good yields ..."

What else did he say?

"Is it?" The forced upbeat tone was obvious and rang hollow.

"Mar'-"

"Don't ... I'll see Medic. By the time you get back, everything will be fine, and we'll try again ..."

"Okay ... What about the baby?"

"A girl ... They didn't let me see her – probably best. You should get ready; the bell will sound soon. I'm going to bed-"

"But-"

"I'm tired, David ..."

In an ever-deepening well of despondency, he picked at the food, cleared away and got ready to leave, conscious of the darkening cloud brewing on the other side of the room.

"I should ask to stay with you ..."

"You know that's impossible – there's no need. I'll have Peter to keep me company and lots of work to do if the *spiro* is, like you say, going great guns ..."

Not only guilty but helpless – he grabbed a shower to have something to do and to escape for five minutes.

"You're sure I can't do anything for you before I leave, Mar'?"

"No; it's fine ... Go and say goodbye to everyone – I'm going to bed."

He kissed her as tenderly as he knew how, but his advances were not met, and Marion deflected his ministrations by fussing with his shirt collar. He picked up the plates to take back and left swiftly, avoiding the path that swung by Peter's and Gwen's dwelling for fear of hearing something he would rather not take to the *cryo* chamber.

By virtue of being ahead of the rest, he got processed early and went to the holding room, happy to not have to speak to anyone in particular.

Nurse was surprised when he presented himself at the Jab Station well ahead of time.

"David?"

"Seems pointless delaying it ..."

"These things happen, David – there are no guarantees. You'll get a permit next time, rest assured."

He knew it only too well.

The needle stung and made him draw a sharp breath.

"Such a baby! – Sorry ... If you're sure, you can go in – don't you want to wait for Gwen, so you get assigned adjacent pods on the same level?"

"Makes no difference, does it?"

"Makes it easier for Marion or Peter if they double up on cleaning duties – up to you ..."

"Put me in – the sooner it starts, the sooner it's over ..."

"You know the drill ..."

He moved to the furthest pod on the highest level. The Tech waved him forward.

"Strip, please ..."

He took off his clothes and put them in the bag provided.

"Get in ..."

He stepped into the pod and squeezed himself into the oddly shaped seat and waited for the cowl to be lowered with its array of monitors. When the cap-shaped moulding touched his head, he spasmed.

"Sorry; systems have been glitching all day."

He smiled wanly, not really paying attention.

"Ready?"

"Yep ..."

"Night, night ..."

The Tech pressed the combi-pen style syringe to his neck and pressed the trigger. The effect was immediate, and he sensed his body slump into the seat.

In the final second, which he always thought was cruel, he felt the feeding and excretion tubes locate and lock, reminding him that he was tethered to life support and completely dependent on the system and as helpless as any baby in its mother's womb – Marion's depressed look was the last thing he remembered before the curtain came down.

Just as the Tech was closing the door of the pod to start flooding it with the *cryo* gas that effectively kept the occupant in a state of suspended animation for the next six months, Peter was urging Gwen to go with him to Marion.

"She won't want to see us, Peter, I'm telling you."

"Don't you want to say goodbye?"

"She's just lost her baby, Peter; have a heart. You'll see her tomorrow anyway ..."

"I just thought she'd appreciate it ... And you can pick up David and walk in together."

"I'll see him in reception ... Okay! I'm ready. Don't walk back; get some rest, yeah?"

"If you're sure ..."

He watched her leave. After five minutes, he quit their dome and ran to the mushroom huts, heading straight for the filtration hub, squatting down behind the big extraction fan unit.

"C'mon, David!"

Seconds later, the first bell sounded. There was still time; no reason to panic or get upset, he told himself.

Only by thinking about the following day and opening up the water cistern to extract their diary did he manage to quell the tears that threatened to spring from his eyes. He even managed a smile.

"What's keeping you?"

A scraping sound caught his attention. He looked up and peered over the edge of the unit, only to see Superintendent exit the grading room and lock up.

The second bell sounded.

"David!"

It was inconceivable that he would miss this – they never missed this last chance to kiss each other goodbye.

He couldn't decide what to do. If he ran back to Dome Town, he might miss him altogether.

"It must be Marion ..."

The conclusion was scant comfort.

He slumped back down and waited for the final bell to sound before resigning himself to the fact that David wasn't coming. When his legs began to cramp up, he moved out and wandered to the courtyard, hoping to see someone who might have seen David.

He was in luck. One of the Tech was taking a break.

"Have you seen David go in?"

"Go in? He was *first* in – an hour ago ..."

Chapter Two – In The Service of Homemaker

When the alarm went off, *reveille* found him awake, staring at the ceiling, and already dressed.

Fear and depression had moulded themselves into numbing disbelief. By rote, he made breakfast, filled his flask, and quit the dome to head to the farm. Without waiting for Marion, he trotted out, ignoring everyone else; most were standing around enjoying the fresh air and the sunshine, patently ignoring Manager's frozen scowl.

Inside the farm, he headed straight for the water cistern and retrieved the book, hoping, maybe praying, that it might shed some light on David's behaviour.

'I'm beyond excited at the prospect of seeing you later. In all honesty, I don't know how much more of this I can take. There is a way out, but I won't go without you. I love you. David.'

He scanned successive previous entries, noticing the increasingly desperate voice.

"There is no *way out* – where the hell does he think we'd go?"

"Peter!"

Caught unawares, he had no chance to hide the book, and rammed it under a pile of mushroom compost, turning and smiling, having recognised the voice as Toby's; someone he was pleased to see.

"Toby!"

"How you doin', fella?"

"I'm good. Why do you talk like a teenager?"

"Well; I figure I only age at half the rate of someone who never gets frozen – so I'm still pretty much a teenager by that reckoning."

"Is that so? What are you doing here?"

"Reassigned while Marion is recuperating ..."

"Oh ... yeah ... In which case, can you empty the drying frames and get set up for the next batch?"

"Sure ... *How was Gwen?*"

He recognised the tone – lewd and wholly inappropriate.

"Much the same as Denise, I'm sure ..."

"Nearly missed the final bell! Have you seen Ronan?"

"No. Why?"

"Amy called for Denise – says he came out and went off without saying a word – not one word."

"Where's he assigned?"

"Hive maintenance. I certainly wouldn't send the guy up a ladder. Where are the harvest trolleys?"

"In sanitization – be quick."

"Yes, boss!"

While Toby fetched the trolleys, he retrieved the book and hid it in the water cistern, plagued by the last entry, wondering, despite everything they had been taught, whether the outside was as truly dangerous as they were told – a flock of questions threatened to take flight but Toby's noisy re-emergence into the unit shut the door on them. For the next few hours, they harvested the *spiro*, re-stocked the drying frames and planted up the next set of trays, ending with all the filtration checks they were required to do before breaking for lunch.

They stepped outside.

"Can you double up and clean Denise's pod for me tomorrow when you do Gwen's?"

"Sure; why?"

"Medical tomorrow ... I'll do it the day after."

"Medical?"

"Applied for R and D – you know how strict they are in there."

"Why do you want to move to Research?"

"Because I'm bored to death doing this for one ... and R and D get automatic privileges."

"But you have no science credits – what's the point?"

"Didn't you ever just want to do something to make a difference?"

"I do – we keep the commune alive; isn't that enough?"

"Ten years of doing this shit – something has to change."

For the rest of their break, Peter kept quiet, feigning a nap, struggling to keep the growing sense of dread at bay.

"What is wrong with everyone?"

Only Manager's visit and a verbal commendation on the yields put the smile back on his face.

"The guy's a creep. Why the fuck should he escape the pod? He does nothing to earn the right ..."

He ignored Toby's comments and started the cleaning of the trays.

When Toby left to collect the plant food; the mix of salts and nitrates that they used to create the growing medium for the *spiro*, he dived back into the book, flicking back to the first entry of David's last outside session.

'Hope the taste of your kiss lasts forever. Gwen talks about nothing except babies!! It's so unfair that we can't be together. I know we must be grateful. Some days, all I want is to have been born a cleaner. I hope you're dreaming of me and not cyanobacteria! I love you. I've always loved you. I will always love you.'

Cleaners: his mind switched back to the sight of the crew that had arrived at lunchtime. He'd spied on the gang, pretending to be asleep, feasting his eyes on their glistening backs and sweat-stained *nyleen* shorts, wondering if the rumours were true, but seriously doubting it.

"Peter!"

"Uh?"

"Wakey-wakey! Help me unload then we can go grab something to eat – c'mon, man!"

He splashed water on his face to wake himself up and try and force his cock to behave itself. Hiding the book again, he scampered to the unloading bay, jostling with Toby, willing himself to forget the look on the youngest crewman's face, who'd stared at him for a minute while the gang had taken a break. It had been a look of pure lust – animalistic, feral, and uncontrollably lustful.

oOo

"Don't look so worried; it's the same for everyone – and you know what they say, as soon as you close your eyes, you're opening them again. Now, look after Gwen, and keep an eye on Amy, will you?"

"I will, Mar', I promise."

"And David ..."

"What?"

"You were amazing last night – so stop worrying so much and just relax."

She'd cum while he was still thrusting into her; he'd thought her cries were of pain. When he'd tried to pull out, she'd clamped her legs around his waist tighter, imploring him to fuck her harder. He couldn't say he'd hated it. He'd tried to imagine if it was how Peter felt when he fucked him – this urge to thrust and eject his seed. He knew he didn't have the urge to fuck Peter as much as he clearly did, wanting – craving – Peter's cock and the sensation of it slipping inside him.

They left the dome to head to the hall ahead of the first time they would be separated. In his eyes, six months felt like an eternity, and with precious little comfort, knowing Gwen would spare him and everyone else none of the details of her last night with Peter. He tried to focus on how Marion must be feeling as she approached her first deep freeze.

He sought out her hand and squeezed it.

"Don't worry ..."

He felt ashamed that she was trying to calm his nerves.

"... Study hard; think of the community and how much everyone depends on us."

He knew *us* meant the farmers.

Who decided such things? Why hadn't he been allocated to Tech or R&D?

"Any idiot can grow *spiro-*"

"No, they can't! It takes skill and experience – anyone can oil a cog ..."

She always did have a knack of being able to read his thoughts.

Before he could answer, the public address system boomed out the order to muster. Soon thereafter, they were swamped by the rest of the couples making their way to registration and processing.

Just as he began to relinquish any hope that he would see Peter before he disappeared into the processing area, he felt the familiar strength of his secret lover's hand grip his shoulder.

Before the sensation had barely registered, it was gone as the crowd whipped Peter away along with Marion, leaving him with Gwen by his side.

"Best we start on cleaning all those frames ..."

"Yes ... Six months-"

"We mustn't think about it too much, David ... We have each other and our friends. We are so much better off than those poor girls and boys destined to clean for the rest of their lives."

He didn't reply. He couldn't deny what she had said. For all the rumours circulating, he still preferred to sleep in a bed in a comfortable dome and eat *A Grade* gloop with the promise of ice cream if they beat the yield targets.

oOo

Once he and Toby had finished up, he followed Toby as far as the mess hall but skipped the line once Toby fell into conversation with one of the girls, and hot-footed it to Marion and David's dome.

He knocked.

After a couple of minutes, Marion appeared at the door.

"Oh; hello, Peter ..."

"How are you? Can I get you anything?"

"I'm fine – really. Won't you come in?"

He stepped tentatively inside, accepting the offered kiss on his cheek.

"I'm so sorry, Marion; truly I am."

"Ours is not to reason why, is it? Once I have the test, hopefully, they will know better, and we'll plan to try again. I'm so sorry I kept Gwen back for so long-"

"Don't be silly ... Are you sure you don't need anything at all?"

"I'm fine. I'll be at the farm tomorrow after lunch. David said the yields are amazing this season ..."

He had to smile at the allusion. Their lives were dominated by the Hive, and nothing ever changed, yet each changeover heralded some kind of renewal, fuelled by perhaps a longed-for wish for a difference. He knew he was too cynical to appreciate it.

"So says the log. If you're sure that you don't need anything, I'll see you tomorrow, Marion."

He left, conscious of the effort to hide his relief at being let off the hook so readily.

Having no appetite to speak of, he wandered to the mushroom tunnels to check on the harvest and to organise the transport of the compost to the unit where some of it was used to manufacture the growing tubes.

The cleaning gang was just finishing up. One of the cleaners, a man of his own age, was tipping the last of the spent compost into one of the big hoppers for wheeling to the factory.

He held back and waited.

The man turned, briefly casting an eye over him before putting his shoulder to the heavy cart. Feeling the keen edge of the man's apparent disdain, Peter loitered, avoiding further eye contact.

"Sikinia!"

The outburst coincided with a loud crash as the cart toppled over, spilling its precious contents all over the courtyard.

The word meant nothing to Peter. He knew the cleaners spoke a different language; he had never bothered to pay it any attention. As a rule, the cleaners were silent when going about their work. On rare occasions, when the crew's superintendent issued an order, the words sounded harsh and made him wince as if he had been stung by a whip.

He would have scurried away to avoid any trouble, but the man appeared injured. Torn between helping the man and making himself scarce, it was only when the man shouted, *"Msaada!"* that he found it impossible to ignore the obvious plea.

He looked about but there was no one else in sight.

"Msaada!"

Then he saw the blood pouring from a cut on the man's arm.

Instinctively, he rushed forward. The man was wearing nothing but *nyleen* shorts, useless for a bandage. Fumbling for any memory of his first aid training, he ripped the arm from his coverall to use it as a tourniquet.

As he reached forward, the cleaner stepped back, evidently afraid.

"Don't worry! We have to stop the bleeding."

Whether it was his tone or just desperation, the cleaner remained still as he wound the fabric around the man's arm and tied it off. Quickly, he ripped off the other arm and used it as a makeshift bandage. By now, and perhaps alerted to the fact that something was amiss by the sound of the trolley falling over, a small knot of the man's co-workers had gathered at the side of the yard. Peter noticed them when the injured man called something out over his shoulder. To his mind, they all looked afraid but also a little curious. Shortly afterwards, the superintendent appeared at the head of the group. He strode over, barking orders to the men. When he reached Peter and the injured man, he spoke more softly and directly to Peter, "Thank you; your assistance is appreciated. The damage to your clothing is most regrettable. Our apologies ..."

Peter was transfixed, not so much by the words themselves but by the submissive, almost fawning tone, and it sounded to him that the man was merely repeating the words by rote with very little idea of their actual meaning.

Before he could reply, Manager appeared at his shoulder.

"What the devil do we have here?"

"Manager! There was an accident; the man was bleeding heavily ..."

Something passed between the two supervisors that Peter interpreted as 'this will not go unpunished'.

"Get cleaned up, Peter. I'll credit you with the lost time. See me later to get a requisition for a new uniform."

Reluctantly, he peeled away from the group and turned to march away but not before catching the injured man's eye and smiling. The man did not respond. To his mind, it was as if the man had withdrawn albeit he was very pale and sweating freely, clearly in shock.

Peter hurried back to the *spiro* farm, where he reported everything to Toby, who was enrapt.

"You *actually* spoke to him; touched him?"

"He was bleeding badly; I couldn't leave him."

"I bet Manager is furious."

"But it was an accident ..."

"I bet we don't see that man again ..."

"What do you mean?"

But Toby side-stepped the question, and dove into his favourite subject being his impending transfer to R&D.

At the end of his shift, he walked quickly to Manager's office to collect his requisition form.

"Ah, Peter; there you are! Come in. Any ill-effects?"

"Ill-effects? I don't understand; I wasn't hurt."

"I meant shock – trauma ..."

"No, nothing like that. Is the man alright?"

Manager coughed and spluttered, barely able to contain his evident surprise, "As far as I know, he is being treated in the clinic ... If you hurry, you'll just make Stores before they close for the evening. My advice is to forget the incident, Peter."

Before he could ask why, Manager stood up and handed Peter the form, practically throwing him out but not before adding, "How is Marion?"

"S-she was fine – a little tired. She's back to work tomorrow, she says."

"Good!"

With which, Manager propelled him outside, kicking the door closed.

Unsure of what to make of Manager's behaviour, he rushed to Stores to requisition another uniform. Even if he could choose to forget the incident, when he entered the dining hall, everyone wanted to know what had happened. Mobbed, it was only Medic's appearance that put paid to an outright riot.

"Come to my office, Peter ..."

He threw a glance at Toby, who just shrugged his shoulders.

Leaving his food untouched, he walked swiftly through the parting crowd.

One of the nurses stopped him before he could enter Medic's office.

"Hold still."

"Wh – OUCH!"

"Always such a baby."

"Why do I need a shot?"

"Just a precaution."

"But I wasn't hurt. I don't under-"

"Peter!"

Medic's call put paid to any further questions. The nurse stepped aside and waved him through to the office.

"Sir; I don't understand-"

"Sit down, young man ..."

He seated himself in the chair opposite the man, who, dressed in his customary white tunic, made Peter acutely aware of his bare arms.

"... Just a precaution because of the blood."

"I didn't get any on my hands."

"Good! Glad to hear it ... Now ... I understand that you saw Marion. How was she?"

"F-fine; just tired. She said she had to have a test."

"Yes; to find out why she lost the baby – deeply upsetting. You and Gwen have had no success in that ... *area* ... Anything wrong?"

He blushed in the face of the question.

"Come now, Peter; don't be coy. We all strive for the future of homestead – everyone must do their bit. If you and Gwen are having any difficulties-"

"We aren't ... It just hasn't happened."

He had done his duty; Gwen had seen to that.

"Perhaps we will requisition a test before the next changeover just to be sure ... If you are sure you are feeling well, I see no reason why you should not return to work tomorrow – and keep an eye on Marion for me, please."

"Yes ... of course."

"Run along then ..."

He excused himself, feeling confused and apprehensive. It wasn't until he got back to the dwelling that he was able to calm down. He glugged down some water and helped himself to a handful of crackers, suddenly aware of just how hungry he was.

As tempted as he was to seek out Marion to ask her what she thought of everything that had happened, he chose instead to have a long hot shower and lay down.

Only when the compound's lights dimmed did he realise just how long he had lain motionless. With no desire to close his eyes, he turned over onto his side to watch the shadows flicker as the window blind swayed to the rhythm of the air being pumped in through the air conditioning vent.

oOo

He was only aware of the fact that he had dropped off when he woke up abruptly, instantly aware of the pounding of his heart.

The silence, save for the gentle whirr of the air pump, was deafening. He breathed deeply for a few minutes to calm his pulse. Feeling the pressure in his bladder, he slipped out of bed and padded to the bathroom to relieve himself.

As he leaned forward and reached out to push the flusher, he heard the unmistakable sound of gravel being crunched underfoot outside the bathroom window. The window was too high to see out of and, in any event, it was frosted for privacy. Padding back through to the main room, he grabbed a knife from the kitchen drawer and crept up to the main door, placing his ear against it

He could hear nothing except for the sound of his blood rushing through his ears. He was certain that he hadn't imagined it. Agreeing with himself that there was only one way to be sure, he cracked the door and peered out through the narrow slit.

He couldn't see anything beyond the edge of the small porch, which cut off his view of the main path. The only sound was the *whoosh* of the main wind turbine, high above his head. Convinced now that he had imagined it, the muffled and far-off sound of a door closing with a definite *thud*, brought everything back into sharp focus. Knowing he'd never settle until he had taken a look around the side of the dome, he squared his shoulders and prepared to step outside.

Brandishing the knife, he slowly pushed the door open, immediately sensing the relative coolness of the night air on his skin. It made him shiver.

He stepped out into the porch, hugging the wall, stopping just short of the edge so that he could peer around it without being seen.

His eyes were already adjusting to the gloom. Beyond his little garden, all he could see were the humps of the other domes in his enclave.

Feeling slightly foolish, he straightened his back and stepped onto the path that ran around the dome. Three strides brought him far enough around the dome so that he could see the bathroom window. Having convinced himself that there was nothing amiss, the flash of silver made his heart skip a beat. He tightened his grip on the knife.

He could hear nothing to account for the little flash of silver, which continued to wink at him.

"What the fuck is going on ...?"

He couldn't say he was afraid. Intrigue, however, got the better of him and he moved forward, holding the knife out in front. Six paces brought him level with the bathroom window, and then he understood why he had been confused. The little silver flash was caused by something suspended from the air conditioning pipe. He reached out with the knife and prodded the object. He heard a faint ting and realised that it was made of metal.

"What-the-fuck?"

He reached out to touch it with his fingers of his other hand. Once his fingers encounter the metal, they automatically enclosed the little square of metal, which was suspended by a thong. For some reason, it felt reassuring. Taking a quick glance over his shoulder first, he slipped the thong off the pipe's clamp and scampered back, securing the door, and locking it for the first time in an age. Beneath the angel-poise lamp that sat above his desk, he brought the object into the light to examine it.

"Oh ... my ..."

oOo

When he'd seen Marion as he'd left the dome for work, she'd told him that she would be no more than an hour. They'd parted at the roadway. He hurried to the *spiro* farm and retrieved the diary, eager to write everything down for David.

And now, for the first time, he began to believe what David had suspected all along. There was something outside the compound, and that something was being hidden from them. He quickly wrote down the brief facts, starting with the accident right up to the point he had hidden the artefact in the void behind the air conditioning vent.

'... I can't believe it. It proves what you have said all along. The question now is, what do we do about it? I must find the cleaner and try and ask him some questions. Maybe I can speak to Ronan. He works for Hive Maintenance. If anyone can see anything, he can from up there. This is too much to take in. I'll try and find out more and I promise I will write everything down ...'

Rather than risk being caught, just in case Marion was quicker than expected, he hid the diary and set to work, all the while, trying to think of a way of seeing the cleaner again.

"Peter!"

"Oh, Marion; you startled me."

"You were miles away ... What's to do?"

"Can you reload the drying frames while I go to the unit and pick up some more tubes?"

"Sure thing."

"How was the test?"

"I won't find out for a week ... I just have to do my best to forget about it ..."

Taking the hint, he strode purposefully out of the farm and headed for the manufacturing unit. It was the place where the tubes were made from the mushroom compost sown with a specific strain of mycelium. He had seen the process, marvelling at how the organism grew into a fine but strong sheet that could be cut up and used not only for the seedling tubes but also, once strengthened with a kind of epoxy, used as a building material.

Recalling that made him recall the lesson, the history lesson, all those years ago, and he wondered why he remembered it in so much detail; probably because David teased him so much about it, even now.

In fact, it had been David who had seen it first, during their first separation. He always thought it had been shown to take everyone's minds off the deathly long days and even longer nights. The grainy, shaky footage showed soldiers fighting in a faraway country, protecting their freedom from an unspeakably cruel enemy. The clearest image was of three men, holed up behind a wall of sandbags, firing their weapons. Each man was dressed in combat gear except for the blond one, who wore just a vest. Around his neck - and Peter wondered how many of the others had noticed it – a medallion, a square of silver, threaded onto a black string.

The video had been part of their *history* lesson. They were the survivors; they alone carried the hopes and dreams of all humanity into the future. The enemy, who had never been named, had been crushed but so little had survived the terrible onslaught. Outside the compound, nothing existed, nothing but stone and dust; everything had been burned by the terrible fires.

They were the lucky ones. They showed their gratitude through their diligence and unswerving obedience. Like Manager said on every occasion 'continuity must be preserved'.

Except now, it was clear that something had survived. What he couldn't work out was why the cleaner – he assumed the cleaner – had risked so much by bringing the medallion to him – and for what reason?

At the factory, he met Manager.

"Have you recovered, Peter?"

"I got a shot; I don't know why-"

"Just a precaution, I am sure ... What did you need?"

"More tubes ..."

The man left him in the foyer while he fetched the tubes. From his vantage point, he could see across the small yard and beyond to the filtration centre and the Disinfectant Store – the same place where he and David had seen the two cleaners fucking, that had answered the all-important question all those cycles ago. He wished he had reason to go there now.

"There you go, Peter."

He left with his mind whirring, thinking of how he might justify a visit to the store.

For the rest of the day, he laboured beside Marion until it was time to go to the mess hall.

"I'm going back to the pod, Peter. I don't much fancy answering questions today. I'll see you tomorrow."

"Can I fetch you some food?"

"Nurse gave me supplements; I'll be fine. You go ..."

He didn't linger any longer than was necessary. He needed to speak to Ronan if the chance presented itself.

In the dining hall, he found Toby and Ronan.

"Where's Marion?" asked Toby.

"She's tired."

"So ..."

"What?"

"How does it feel to be a hero?"

"Are you serious? I didn't do anything."

"That's not what we all heard – I don't know how you could suffer to be so close."

"They are just like us, Toby."

"If you say ... For all that, it's the most exciting thing that's happened in a very long time."

"How is maintenance, Ronan?"

He timed the question to catch Ronan's eye, who habitually had his head bowed.

"It's fine, just fine ... There is nothing more important than keeping the Hive functioning ..."

They were both used to his slower way of speaking, assuming, like everyone else, that it was a consequence of the medication.

"... I like the ladders; no one else likes to climb so high but I do."

"But there's nothing to see!"

He was sure that he wasn't meant to see the look, but Ronan's eyes seemed to smile in response to Toby's outburst, almost as if he were keeping something secret.

"You can see the whole compound, can't you, Ronan?"

"Everything ... all the way to the Defences ..."

And even though Ronan hadn't had said them, he could swear he heard the words 'and beyond'.

After dinner, he returned to the pod and retrieved the medallion from its hiding place. There was no doubt that it was the same as the medallion worn by the blond soldier in the video. What could not be seen in the video because it was too small and fuzzy were the words engraved on one side of the medal -

'In The Service Of Homemaker'

On the other side, now hard to see because the surface was so worn, was a name, written in little raised dots –

'Noble Scholar'

"*Noble Scholar* ... Is that his name?"

Until well into the evening, he could not think of anything else except the blond soldier, bunkered down behind the wall, shooting his gun, and when he finally closed his eyes, his dreams were filled with smoke and bright flashes of light someway off in the distance, and the image of the man walking towards him, reaching out, smiling as if somehow immune to the destruction all around him.

Chapter Three - The Hive

Desperate to come up with some way to visit the Disinfectant Store, he quit the dome and ran to the Hive to clean and check both Gwen's and David's pods, hoping the routine would give him some inspiration if not peace of mind. At the entrance to the Hive, he met Ronan, who was polishing the windows of the ground floor office suite, above which, fifteen storeys high, the Hive sat like a huge clutch of smooth, white eggs.

"Ronan!"

"Peter ..."

"Are you going up the ladders today? You're so lucky; I've always wanted to see from the top ..."

He was hoping to see that same look, the same poorly guarded smile of the eyes that suggested there was something to see beyond the defence wall that stood as high as the Hive, encircling the compound.

If there was anything, it was interrupted by the noisy exit of three technicians, which sent Ronan scuttling off.

He walked into the foyer to sign the book before ascending to David's level first being the furthest away.

The broad, curved, walkway wound its way around the structure like a coiled spring. On every floor, there was a landing, giving access to the chambers, themselves arranged in a three-tier circle, supported by a framework of gantries and steep staircases.

He found David's pod easily enough and set about cleaning the housing and wiping all the wires and conduits, finishing with the essential bio-checks. He filled in the card that sat in a *plasto* holder beside the pod and signed his name. As always, before he left, he stood in silent contemplation of the cryo chamber and imagined David inside, sleeping soundly.

"If there is an out there, I'd rather live for one second in it with you than live a lifetime separated like this ..."

oOo

They spent the day cleaning trays and scrubbing out the spare drying machine given that yields were so good.

"We're going to need it, Peter. I spoke to Manager while you were at the Hive. Thank you for cleaning today; I'll do it tomorrow."

"I don't mind ... Is that all the soap we have?"

"Yes ..."

His heart skipped a beat and the hairs on his arms stood on end.

"I'll ask Manager for a requisition ... There is entertainment tonight ..."

"Don't tell me; the usual film?"

"Better than none and there'll be ice cream ... Won't you come?"

"I suppose so ..."

Anything to see Ronan again.

At the end of their shift, he rushed to catch Manager and obtain the necessary requisition before joining Marion in the hall. It was packed. She had, of course, been commandeered by the usual gaggle of young women, leaving him to find a seat with Toby and Ronan.

"We've seen this film a hundred times!"

"Stop complaining, Toby ... Fetch the ice cream."

"Yes, sir!"

It was a deliberate ploy to get Ronan to himself albeit for just a few minutes.

"How was your day, Ronan?"

"I cleaned all the glass ..."

"Well done ..."

He found it hard not sound patronising although he was never sure if Ronan truly paid attention to anything that anyone said.

"... I would love to go to the top of the Hive ..."

"On Founders' Day, you could volunteer and help me raise the pennant ..."

Why hadn't he thought of it himself?

"I'll speak to Manager then ..."

When nothing else appeared to be forthcoming, he settled back in his seat. When Toby got back, he accepted his ice cream and then pretended to be engrossed in the film, in truth, rehearsing his request for the privilege to help Ronan, knowing that, usually, one of the girls was chosen.

Once the film had ended, everyone returned to their domes. At the head of the path to Peter's, Ronan stopped.

"Can I ask you something, Peter?"

"Of course."

"Can we go inside?"

"Sure ..."

Though not forbidden, visits were not encouraged. Once inside the dome, Peter drew off some water and motioned to Ronan to sit down at the small dining room table.

"What did you want to ask me?"

It was painfully obvious, from the pause, that a battle royale was being waged inside the man's head. Peter waited patiently, knowing Ronan often found it hard to make himself understood.

"What if ... What if some of the things we have been told weren't true ..."

"What things, Ronan?" He deliberately kept his tone even, almost deadpan, not wishing to cause any undue agitation. Despite that, he felt queasy and a cold sweat broke out on his face; shuddering, all the hairs on his arms went up.

He took a seat opposite Ronan, willing the man to look him in the eye.

"Do you remember what was said in our history lesson about the Great Fire?"

He didn't have to think very hard. So little was known about the past that their history lessons had barely filled a semester.

"It destroyed everything except for the land here where the compound was built by our Founders ..."

"What if that wasn't true; what if there was something outside the compound?"

"Like what, Ronan? Have you seen something with your own eyes?"

Had he seen something from the top of the ladder? But from his memory of the defences, the top of the Hive was level with the encircling wall.

"When you stand on the *very* top of the Hive and look out towards the place where the sun sets, you can just see it-"

"What? What can you see, Ronan?"

"Do you remember in the film when the children leave the forest and come across the windmill?"

"Yes ..."

"It's like the top of the sail of the windmill but narrower and shiny ..."

"Does it turn?" Peter asked, remembering how, in the film, when the wind blew, the sails of the windmill turned, and the miller ground the flour for the bread.

"I cannot say ... but it is real, and it is there ..."

Peter sat back, astounded but also deeply sceptical until he remembered something from the old footage of the soldiers fighting.

"Do you remember the old history lesson film with the soldiers?"

"Yes ..."

"Do you remember that they were holed up behind the wall of sandbags, but in the distance, on the ground, is the burnt-out hulk of the wind turbine?"

"Sort of ... It could be a blade, I suppose ... But how is it there?"

"I don't know ... Maybe something survived. How far away do you think it is?"

"The defence wall is five kilometres from the centre of the compound ... at least as far again, if not further – it is very, very small but unmistakable."

"It could not be a trick of the light?"

"No; I have seen it more than once ... I must go or questions might be asked ..."

Ronan left, leaving Peter deep in thought. The two events, the discovery of the medallion and Ronan's disclosure, could not be unconnected was his first conclusion. Maybe somehow the cleaner had found the medallion, but that would mean that the man had been outside the walls.

In that moment, thoughts began to unravel like when he pulled out the big hose to wash down the yard.

"Do *they* come from the outside?"

He knew that the gangs did not go into *cryo*. He just assumed – had always assumed – that they lived out their lives in their compound. He felt guilty for thinking so little of them, thinking so little about them.

"Is that what he was trying to say to me?"

More convinced than ever that the medallion had been left by the cleaner whom he had helped, he knew he had to do two things: visit the disinfectant store and try to speak to him and get to the top of the Hive with Ronan.

When he went to sleep, which did not come easily, he lay in bed with the medallion in his hand, finding it strangely comforting in light of the alarming thought that, they were not alone, and maybe had never been alone.

oOo

He had his requisition; Marion had agreed to do the cleaning. His visit to the store had to be timed to perfection and coincide with the cleaners' break. He'd woken up in a pool of sweat; his dreams had tormented him all night – dreams of reaching out and always finding the thing he was reaching for, just out of his grasp. Sometimes, it was the medallion, other times, the wind turbine blade, most often, David's outstretched hand.

He showered, happy to be clean and refresh.

He strode to the farm, checked the numbers, and then found the two pails that held the soap, which needed to be refilled. He thought about writing in the diary, but his hands were shaking just a little. He'd been tempted to carry the medallion but, in the end, he had hidden it again, not wanting to risk losing it or someone discovering it.

Minor tasks occupied an hour. He got ready to leave just as Marion arrived.

"I won't be long, Marion – everything is done."

"Thank you, Peter. Could you also requisition some new trays; I noticed a few were cracked. I'll commission the new drying frame in the meantime ..."

He wanted to tell her, but he couldn't garner his thoughts or risk uncapping his emotions. He left swiftly, and jogged to the store, praying that the cleaners were on their break. Their yard was just beyond the store.

Masking his true intent, he handed in his chit and waited for the pails to be refilled. Then, when the tech returned them to him, he 'remembered' the trays. The tech huffed and complained that he was late for his break.

"I'll get them; I've had mine."

"In the shed at the back of the yard; don't touch anything else." With which, the tech rushed off, leaving Peter alone. He took a minute to compose himself, breathing deeply. When he felt calm, he stepped out into the yard and walked to the rear shed, closing the door behind him. At the rear of the shed, behind the stack of trays, was a window, always left cracked to keep the trays from sweating. He squeezed in behind the trays and inched closer to the window. Using his sleeve, he buffed the window and looked out, rewarded by the sight of the crew, lounging in the yard. He scanned them, picking out the man he had helped, who was easy to identify, being bandaged up. The white bandage stood out against the tanned skin, giving Peter plenty of reasons to swallow hard, remembering the scene from years ago of the two men fucking like dogs.

He stood still for a moment.

Knowing that the 'break over' bell would sound very soon, he pumped himself up and pushed the window open, making as much noise as possible. None of the men except for a younger pair paid any attention.

"For pity's sake, look round, damn you!"

Time was running out. In desperation, he swung it right back until it clanged against the stop. All the men looked around. He made out like he was looking for something but still managed to throw a glance in the man's direction.

He prayed that the man understood.

The bell rang, and the men all got up to leave.

"Shit!"

He knew only one word of their language; the word the man had cried out when he had cut himself.

"Msaada ... msaada!"

As the rest of the men filed out of the yard, he circled and approached the window, keeping his head down.

Without raising his head, the man said, "*Uku* ... t-o-n-i-g-h-t ... *djumba* ... h-o-m-e ..."

Before Peter could question what the man had said, he ran off, barely catching up the rest before the last man had exited the yard gate.

The clang of the gate slamming shut propelled him into action. He closed the window to, picked up the trays and headed out, bumping into the tech who was coming back from break. To divert attention, he asked him to borrow a trolley.

"Remember to bring it back!"

"Thank you ..."

He wheeled the trolley, piled up with the pails and the trays back to the farm.

"What took so long? You missed break!"

"The tech was on break when I got there; I had to wait."

"Let's get the machine loaded and tested ..."

For once, he appreciated Marion's direction and the fact that she didn't want to talk very much. Only when she went to see Manager to ask him to calibrate the machine, did he risk extracting the diary from its hiding place. He scribbled a few lines before she returned with Manager.

The job of calibrating the machine was a job of mere minutes. Before Manager turned to leave, Peter asked him about the Founders' Day fete and the possibility of raising the pennant with Ronan.

"By rights, it should be one of the girls – Marion this time in fact. If she doesn't want to do it, you can ... Marion?"

"I don't mind if Peter wants to do it ..."

"Thank you."

"That's settled then ... Clean up in here and take the rest of the day as a free period. Well done!"

oOo

Once everything had been cleaned down, Marion headed off to her dome while Peter rushed to the library. Free time was a rarity and not to be questioned only enjoyed.

He had a pass and privileges, being a farmer. The librarian didn't query his appearance.

He grabbed some books on hydroponics and then skirted the end of the aisle to slip into the section on ancient languages. It was seldom used, and the rows of books were dusty.

He had no idea where to begin.

There were dictionaries but he didn't know what language the cleaners spoke among themselves – the realisation that he knew practically nothing was quickly dawning on him.

He heard the scrape of a chair and scurried back to his own section just in time. The librarian appeared with the trolley of returned books.

"You're the one who helped the cleaner, are you not?"

"I-I did ... he cut himself; I bandaged his arm ... Strange language they speak. I could not understand him although it was clear he was calling for help – *msaada!*"

"It is an ancient language called *Ngazidja* ..."

"Fascinating ..."

"I'm heading to lunch early; can you make sure you close the door when you leave?"

"Yes, of course ... Thank you ..."

Only once he heard the librarian's retreating steps in the corridor outside did he move swiftly back to the section of languages. It took a few minutes to find a dictionary. He looked up *msaada* and confirmed what he thought it meant, "... *help* ..."

Slipping the book in between the others, he moved a book from the bottom shelf up and in its place to camouflage its absence, and then he scanned the barcodes of the books he wanted to borrow and logged them out to his number, and left quickly, avoiding the food hall, and headed straight home. Only when the door was closed behind him did he breathe easier.

After confirming that the medallion was still in its hiding place, he munched his way through a pile of crackers and downed a jug of water to wash the metallic taste of spent adrenalin out of his mouth before sitting down at the table to study the dictionary.

"... U-k-u ... and he said *tonight* ..." and sure enough, the dictionary confirmed it, "... d-j-u-m-b-a, meaning *home* ... He came here before and left the medallion, didn't he?"

Thinking ahead, he made a list of words that he thought could be useful, and then hid the book, fearing Ronan or Marion might make a surprise entrance. Vainly, he studied the other books, if only to eat away the hours. Feeling anxious and as if ants were crawling over his skin, he decided to go for a run around the perimeter of the compound. Changing into shorts and a vest top, he slipped his feet into lighter shoes for running, and headed out, literally running into Toby.

"Whoa! What's this?"

"Exercise, Toby ... You should join me."

"Far more important things to do."

"Like what?"

"That *spiro* must rot your brain ... Taking care of business, my friend."

"Why would you tell me that, you disgusting dog!"

"Don't tell me you have never *poked your nose into someone else's business*."

"What?!"

"If we do it this week then it's assumed that the coupling at the changeover was successful – no one questions it."

"Who?"

"That would be telling, but she's got blonde hair and works in the kindergarten-"

"Sophia-"

"Shush, *dummkopf!*"

"I hope Eric never finds out. Get out of here."

He'd heard the same rumours as everyone else but had never given it any thought. Shaking his head, he jogged to the start of the marked-out track to warm up.

Curtis was getting ready for a run too, and he debated if some company would be a good thing or not. Deciding it would seem odd if he shunned the invitation, he agreed and proposed to set the pace.

"Kick it up, Peter; I need to burn off some energy."

Their pace effectively stymied much in the way of conversation. Halfway around, Curtis dropped out, leaving Peter to complete the circuit by himself. He was relishing the burn. At the point where the track passed closest to the defences, he stopped to catch his breath. The smooth *plastocrete* wall rose high above his head. He'd volunteered for defence maintenance a few times in the past. Though it never rained now, they always cleared the gullies and culverts in case of flooding. As he recovered, he scanned the terrain, ever hopeful of finding a truly wild plant, and noticed that the grill of the drain hole nearest to him was askew.

"Odd ..."

He stepped forward, intent on just pushing the grill back so that it sat neatly in the retaining frame. Only when the cover wouldn't budge did he bend down to investigate the cause.

"Oh, crap ..."

Suddenly paranoid that a hundred pairs of eyes were watching his every move, he darted off along the track, pushing the pace until he was practically sprinting in the end. When he reached the start point again, he collapsed, deafened by the sound of his heart pounding in his chest and the blood rushing through his ears.

Only when someone's shadow blotted out the sun did he open his eyes. It was Manager.

"Impressive ..."

"Hello, Manager."

"Report to the office after a shower – don't worry; it's nothing to get concerned about. I just want to give you the instructions for raising the pennant on Founders' Day ... Well done."

"Thank you ..."

It was a good fifteen minutes before he felt able to get to his feet. He hobbled to the dome to shower and get dressed. Marion was in her garden.

"Peter; whatever have you been doing?"

"I did a circuit; pushed myself a little too much. I have to go to the office to find out what to do on Founders' Day. Are you okay?"

"Yes; I was tidying up the garden ... For a farmer, David never thinks to weed the beds at home!"

"None of us do!"

"Did he by chance, lend you the digging fork?"

"The digging fork? No; I don't think so ... Why?"

"It's missing. I can only assume it's broken. I just don't understand why he wouldn't have replaced it ..."

"Let me lend you ours ..."

His heart was beating so hard that he was sure it was going to burst out of his chest. He retrieved the fork from his and Gwen's cubby and gave it to Marion.

When he'd read in the diary -

'I'm beyond excited at the prospect of seeing you later. In all honesty, I don't know how much more of this I can take. There is a way out, but I won't go without you. I love you. David.'

He had assumed it was just the ravings of a lunatic. Now he knew the truth and the knowledge was more frightening than anything he'd seen or heard in his life.

"You seem distracted, Peter ..."

"Wh ... No; just thinking about Founders' Day ... I must get to the office ..."

It gave him some respite, having to get himself into some kind of shape to see Director. It was a rare enough event. After showering and dressing in clean clothes, he stepped to the office and reported to reception. While he waited, he feigned interest in the yield statistics that were plastered over the walls.

"Come through, Peter, please ..."

Director's assistant held the door open for him.

"Thank you."

"Take a seat; Director will be with you shortly ... May I fetch you some water?"

"Oh; yes. Thank you ..."

He clasped his hands in his lap to stop himself from fidgeting. A few minutes after the assistant brought him some water, Director made his appearance. He had only seen the man this close once before. He found it difficult to age him; he supposed he must be in his fifties.

"Yields are superb, Peter – we will need to commission a third drying machine at this rate!"

He wondered if the comment was designed purely to make him think that the man was genuinely interested in their work. He didn't look as if he'd ever eaten *spiro* in his life; the man's weight was carefully masked by the well-tailored suit, but the flaccid jowls could not be camouflaged.

"We do seem to have found the right formula ... I put my name forward for the honour of raising the pennant on Founders' Day with Ronan."

"Yes, so I hear. Good man for volunteering, seeing as Marion is probably not up to the task this time given the circumstances ... I'm happy to approve your request, Peter ... Tell me, how was David when you saw him at changeover? I got the impression that he was somewhat depressed even before Marion's news ..."

This felt staged. The words were spoken casually enough but their ring was hollow in his ears. The hairs went up on his neck.

"He didn't say very much to me about anything ... He seemed okay. Maybe he was just worried about Marion's pregnancy."

"It is only natural for a father to be worried – it is a damned blow but there is always next time ... How are you and Gwen doing?"

The comment managed to slip in under his radar and he blurted back, "We're fine!"

"No need to worry; it is exceedingly rare that we intervene in a couple's ... how shall I put it ... lack of success? Work hard, rest and study ... Nature takes her own course. As for the Founders' Day service, speak to Manager about timings. Thank you, Peter ..."

He assumed he was dismissed and got up from his seat.

"... I haven't thanked you for assisting one of the cleaning crew; it is noted ... but it is always worth remembering that contact with the cleaning crews should always be kept to a minimum ..."

"Thank you, Director ..."

Was it a warning? Did they know something?

He was sure not; else he was convinced something would have already been said. He headed back to the dome to sit down and think.

When he returned, he found the digging fork by his door. It triggered another set of thoughts.

"Why the hell did he risk it?"

He tried to put the image out of his head, but it was impossible. When he had inspected the drain cover more closely, he'd seen the digging fork at the bottom of the drainage pit. The idea that David had started to dig his way out was both crazy and frightening.

There was little to do before lights out; he weeded his garden, spurred on by Marion's barb, and cleaned the other tools for the sake of something to do. He skipped dinner and read some more of the dictionary. It was strangely soporific, and by the time lights out came, he was fast asleep, slumped over the table.

oOo

He'd have cried out if there hadn't been a hand clamped over his mouth. His whole body jolted, and the chair kicked back but hit something solid. Just as he started to panic, he heard the lilting voice again, *"Rua!"*

Instinctively, he fought to free himself from the arms that encircled his chest, but he grew calmer quickly.

"Mi uparwa Ali Ben ..."

It helped when he recognised the words. He slumped a little and the man dropped his hand.

"M-i u-p-a-r-w-a Peter ..."

He sensed the man's relief. He turned to see the man's face. Although it was dark in the dome, he could still make out the strong jawline, and the bandage glowed supernaturally.

"*Barza ...*"

It was hard to concentrate for the strong scent of fresh sweat and the glint of a smile.

"*B-a-r-z-a ... K-a-n-t-s-i ...*"

The man took the offered seat. Peter pushed the water jug in the man's direction. Without any ceremony, the man picked it up and drained it.

"*Asanta ...*"

He didn't know the word he wanted to use so he tried something close to its meaning, "*I-n-y-i f-u-r-a-h-a?*"

The man smiled but it wasn't patronising, "*Radhi ...* Content, yes."

Peter smiled, relieved. However, he did not know what to do next. As if reading his mind, the man put his hand to his throat.

"Yes; I found it! Sorry! Wait ..."

He got up and the man flinched.

"It's okay – *k-i-d-a-n-i ...*" It was the nearest translation he had found. The word meant necklace. The man nodded. Peter fetched the medallion and put it on the table, asking, "*N-d-a?*"

"Where? *Hule ... hule ...*"

He didn't know the word. He picked up the dictionary, but it was really too dark to see. The man grabbed his attention and gestured with his hand, pointing out of the window but seemingly trying to indicate far away.

"*N-a-m-n-a d-j-e?*"

The man shook his head and Peter knew it was because he could not express himself.

"*U-p-a-r-i-s-a-?*"

"Not find ... *Mililki.*"

"*M-i-l-i-k-i ...* Not understand-"

But before he could say anything else, they heard a noise outside. Peter skipped to the window and pulled back the blind a little. He could see nothing definite, maybe the retreating shadow of Marshal. He kept watch for half a minute, straining to pick up anything else. When he turned back, the man had disappeared.

"Hey!" he cried out in a whisper.

The man stepped out from within the shadows of the alcove beside the closet.

The little bit of extra light illuminated him; a dark glistening body against the uniform white of the *plastocrete* wall. And the bandage made it look as if the man's hand was somehow suspended in thin air. And when that hand reached forward, rather than recoiling, Peter stepped forward and reached out to touch the outstretched fingers.

oOo

The snatched moments with David replayed as an endless loop; they provided the perfect rhythm to the pounding he received from the man who, without ceremony, had slipped of his *nyleen* shorts and had merely gestured to David to lie face down on the bed. Taken so savagely was thrilling, he had to admit as the man's head had probed and then entered him quickly, making his wince and gasp; clenching up had only made it more painful until the pummelling had slowly opened him up until the man's thighs were slapping against his buttocks in time to the ragged breaths that he heard in his head.

Unable to get on top of the feeling, he floundered, fighting for control, which only made the man pound harder. He prayed it would end soon but secretly craved more, and knowing the men's appetites, wondered if one round would be all that was offered.

He needn't have speculated. The man came in a series of bucks that forced Peter further towards the headboard. He braced himself, grabbing fistfuls of the sheets. But no sooner had the man finished pumping him full, he started again, clamping one hand down on the back of his neck and forcing the other under his pelvis to grasp his sack, which he squeezed hard.

The cries got log-jammed in his throat; he barely had the wherewithal to breathe through the pain of having his sack milked so savagely.

Expecting the man to finish quickly, he soon learned that his appetite was far from being sated. Eventually, the man slowed, releasing his grip on Peter's sack in the process. The relief caused him to shoot cum everywhere. But before he could gather his senses, the man began to finger him roughly. Trying to squirm away from the invasion, he only sought to drive the man to force more of his hand inside until he had no choice but to relinquish any control and allow him to fist him until his whole body spasmed.

oOo

Despite being keenly aware of the man's gaze as he cleaned up and hobbled around to find something to wear, he couldn't look him in the eye, not until he had recovered his senses and regained some control.

He had wanted to ask so many questions. When he tried again, the man stopped him by placing his finger to his lips, then pointed to his wrist, and drew two imaginary circles.

"Two days?"

"Two days ... come back ..."

He nodded, readying himself to crawl into bed and hug the pillow to his stomach, sensing the gathering waves of guilt that were looming larger and larger on the horizon.

The man got up to leave. Peter struggled to his feet.

The man stepped forward, towards the door. Peter put out his hand. In a surprisingly tender move, the man picked it up and kissed it.

"*Lala unono* ... two days."

"G-goodbye then ..."

And as quick as lightning, the man disappeared.

He threw himself on the bed, dragging the pillow to hug against his chest, drawing up his knees to make himself as small as possible, willing the waves to overlook him but it was a vain hope, and when they crashed, he was submerged, finding himself inside a Hive pod, able to see out but unable to make himself heard, and David was looking down on him as if he were dead.

oOo

"You look terrible; whatever is the matter? Shouldn't you go and see Medic?"

"I'm fine - really. I just didn't sleep that well – I probably overdid it yesterday on the running track."

He hoped that would put paid to further questions. He did feel wretched, but it was mostly the pain that seemed to dissect his body from the top of his head to the ends of his toes. He didn't need to think long to know where the centre of that pain was – yet, despite the hours of guilt-ridden tossing and turning, he secretly nurtured the feeling that he hadn't felt for years, one of being completely whole.

They worked hard all morning, in fact, he did more than he needed to.

"Slow down, Peter!"

"Director said he was getting us a third drying machine."

"If there is much more to do, they'll need to double the shift crew ..."

He hadn't even thought about it, and then he panicked that someone might find the diary.

"... Peter; you look awfully pale. I think you should see Medic ..."

He fought off the idea until Manager came by and insisted that he go to the medical centre. After the usual tests, the nurse gave him a shot.

"I'm signing you off for two days; you're counts are low. Just rest: it's probably the post-awakening slump – happens to the best of you. Now scoot!"

He stumbled back to the farm to tell Marion what the nurse had said, and then excused himself, staggering back to the dome to fall straight back into his unmade bed. His eyes were closed before his head touched the pillow.

When he woke up hours later, he found a tray of food on the table and a short note from Marion –

'Eat!'

He smiled, trying to visualise her face as she'd encounter the mess and the stink. He ate and then cleaned the dome from top to bottom, stripping the bed and bagging the sheets with the towels for dropping off.

He felt better, albeit still sore.

Thoughts came back to him.

"I have to move the diary ..."

The ones that remained unvoiced all centred on the drain and the digging fork. He had to wonder why David hadn't mentioned it in the diary, but he guessed it was too much of risk to commit it to paper in case someone found it.

"Why didn't he say something?"

He knew the reason; the idea was too big to contemplate – the thought of leaving the compound was terrifying.

oOo

"It's simple, really. When we're both in position, we unfurl the pennant; the cheer goes up ... Nothing to it."

Ronan had called by to make sure he was okay and going to be fit to participate in the ceremony at the end of the week.

"Sounds easy ... Can we go up to practice?"

"I don't see why not ... Have you thought about what I said?"

"About the turbine? Yes ..."

Did he risk telling Ronan what he thought he knew and about the partly dug tunnel?

"If we go up tomorrow just before sunset, you'll see it ... I'll square it with Manager."

"Ok, great."

"Are you okay then? Marion was concerned."

"I'm okay. The nurse gave me a shot. I just have to rest a bit."

"When we're up there, I want to show you something else ... It explains some things."

"What, Ronan?"

"Later; I have to go and finish cleaning the mess hall down. I'll see you tomorrow, ok?"

"Yes ... Take care."

Had David seen something to make him want to leave so badly?

All he knew for certain was what he'd managed to glean from *Ali Ben* – the medallion had come from the outside, and then he remembered the word that *Ali Ben* had used before the noise had disturbed them, "*M-i-l-i-k-i* ..."

He looked it up.

"What is he talking about? Acquired? Purchased?"

He had assumed that the man had found it; if the thought of leaving was terrifying, the thought that there were other people, people outside, was paralysing.

It wasn't uncommon for other halves to do it; he left the dome and went to the Hive to see Gwen. Something about the cool, dark space was oddly comforting just then. He sat beside her pod and laid his head on the surface, pressing his ear to the cool *plasto*, imagining that the faraway humming was somehow her breathing or heartbeat. He was by no means the only one – more of the other halves did the same in the weeks after changeover before the separation became a numbness, and the routine became its own special kind of anaesthesia.

His mind drifted; he desperately wanted to forget the medallion and the cleaner and what Ronan had seen – ignorance was bliss. He scolded himself for being so lazy, so selfish, and so afraid. He didn't want to forget everything else – Gwen, the time spent with David, the satisfaction of knowing that he – amongst others – kept everyone fed. If there were things that he did not understand that was okay for now because he did his job. He even searched out the conduits carrying the pipes and wires that kept half of the community alive for six months of the year. If history lessons filled but a semester, the future filled the rest of the curriculum. The endless lectures on the systems and why they were so important – the blood recycling machine that harvested the antibodies they all needed to survive, the waste recycling – most of which found its way into the mushroom growing medium. He screwed up his nose as he always did when he thought about it. The flow of oxygen and most importantly, the generation of energy to keep everyone alive – he couldn't help himself and thought of Ronan and the wind turbine, and the cleaner and the medallion, knowing he had to have answers … and what did he do with the knowledge that somehow, David had started to dig a way out?

'The facility is closing in five minutes!'

He gathered his senses and stood up, stretching out, before bending over to kiss the pod, whispering, "Goodnight, Gwen." He wished he had the strength to visit David, but curfew saved him further angst; he knew if he had visited the pod, he would have found it hard not to have pounded the pod with his fists and screamed, *'what the fuck are you doing?'*

Ronan was waiting patiently for everyone to leave so he could close up.

"Goodnight, Ronan."

"G-goodnight, Peter … P-Peter …"

He turned.

"… I need to speak to you."

"Come to the dome …"

"Okay …"

He didn't know why they were whispering.

He whiled away a few minutes by making the bed and tidying up his clothes before sitting down to read, or at least, try. His hand absently toyed with the edge of the dictionary and his thoughts returned to *Ali Ben* again and again; the memory of the invasion made him clench up involuntarily. For some reason, despite feeling ashamed, his eye roved over the bed, now made, replaying the scene, recalling, because it was the strongest association, the man's scent - a heady mix of that awful disinfectant, the mushroom compost, day-old sweat, and his sex, the purest essence of his sex. He found himself getting hard and it was only Ronan's arrival that broke the spell.

"Come in, Ronan ... Won't you sit down?"

"Thank you ... Something happened today, and I can't process it. It seems so trivial a thing ... *Spiro* yields have improved have they not?"

"Tremendously. We're commissioning a third drying machine. What has that got to do with anything?"

"I clean all the windows, including the executive suite – you saw Director today; did he approve the plan?"

"Yes, he did ..."

"Excellent! *I* saw Director today, but he did not see me – I was cleaning the ducting that runs beneath his window, and his window was open – not much, but enough for me to hear everything he was saying. I heard a conversation that I do not understand ..."

Peter thought it likely that most people would not understand Director's conversations; he always seemed so remote and ill at ease compared to Manager or Medic.

"... It was unclear to me who he was speaking to – it wasn't Manager or Medic – I thought it was Manager at first because he was talking about yields, but then he said something that did not make sense ..."

"Did you not see the other person?"

"No ... he was alone, but he was speaking, using a communicator thing like the one that Manager has on his desk that he uses when he needs to make an announcement, except this box was not broadcasting what he said so that we could all hear him – it was private ..."

"What did he say about yields or *spiro*?"

"He said – and I could have got this wrong, but it sounded like ... yields are up ... up by one hundred per cent ... yes; I thought you would be pleased ... delivery as usual ... What does he mean *delivery as usual*?"

"Delivery as usual? We deliver the *spiro* to the processing plant ... Manager knows that."

"Then he wasn't speaking to Manager ..."

Did he tell him about the medallion or the partly dug tunnel? These things all felt connected to the wind turbine. Treading cautiously, not knowing Ronan well enough to trust his judgement or discretion, he said, "Listen some more if you can."

"I'll try ... We must be careful. Manager keeps an eye on me because of what happened ..."

"But that was a long time ago, Ronan."

"I know. I don't like it any more than I did but it's easier now."

Peter didn't want to mention the drugs and just smiled.

"I should go. We will practise raising the pennant tomorrow – be at the mess hall just before dinner. If we go up when everyone else is eating, I can show you something else and no one will see ... Goodnight, Peter."

"Goodnight, Ronan ..."

It was late but sleep seemed so far off. He looked out to see Toby slinking back from someone else's dome.

"Psst!"

Toby's head shot around, and once he'd caught sight of Peter, he dived in.

"Don't tell anyone."

"Of course, not ... Who?"

"That would be telling ... You okay?"

"Yeah; I'm okay – just needed to rest. If Marshal had caught you-"

"He won't ... I can't believe you haven't done it."

"Does everyone?"

"A few ... I don't see the issue; we make more babies ..."

He didn't want to think about it but, in spite of himself, and probably due to Toby's heat and the smell of his sweat and the unmistakable edge of fresh cum, he found himself getting hot and partly aroused.

"Water?"

"Yeah; thanks ..."

He grabbed the jug and stepped over to the faucet, and when he turned around, he was aware of Toby's scrutiny.

"What?"

"It doesn't always have to be a girl, you know ..."

He feigned ignorance, "What doesn't?"

"Don't act dumb ... I see the way you look at *certain people*, including me."

"I don't!"

"You do and it's cool ... I guess I have an above-average appetite ..."

"I guess you must ..."

"You're telling me that you never thought about it?"

"I ... I'm not saying that I've never thought about it ..."

"You want me to suck your dick? -"

"Toby!"

"What? Why are you so uptight? No one ever said it was wrong – they never said it was right either but as far as I am concerned, whatever gets you through the day – *and night*."

It was true that no one ever said it was wrong. Sex education had been rudimentary at best and he guessed that the authorities just assumed that everyone just talked about it anyway.

"I'm okay ... Thanks."

"Whatever ... Anytime you feel the need just ask ... I gotta be going. Are you working tomorrow?"

"Another day of rest."

"Great. Means I'm stuck in the farm with *Miss Cheerful-*"

"Toby! She lost her baby."

"I know! For some reason, whenever she sees me, all she wants to do is talk about it!"

"Because she can't talk to David."

"Does she talk to you?"

"Some ... I'll see you later, yeah?"

"For sure. Sure you don't want me to."

Toby got up from the table and brushed past him, grazing his groin with his hand.

"Get out!"

He couldn't settle once Toby had left and he repeatedly beat off but got no release. Bathed in sweat, wound up like a spring, it wasn't until the skies started to brighten that he finally dropped off.

oOo

"Just follow me, using the same hand and footholds, okay?"

"No problem ..."

He'd met Ronan outside the mess hall just as everyone else had finished piling inside. Marion had caught up with him and asked him to sit with her to which he'd replied, "I won't be long ..."

Ronan stepped up first, scaling the first level with ease because it was the shortest and broken into three stepped platforms. The second and third were harder going because there was no break. At the top of the fourth, they rested.

"On Sunday, one of us will have to carry the pennant – it's in a pack and has a strap that you can put over your shoulder like a carryall."

"I don't mind doing it ..."

They laboured up the fifth and sixth and seventh levels, feeling the air freshen with every rung until the wind began to tug at their hair and loose shirts.

"Top of the eighth, it gets harder because the walls bow out more – be careful!"

His calves and biceps ached but it felt good to be doing something different, dare he say, exciting. At the top of the tenth, there was a narrow platform and they rested again and turned and looked out over the compound. Peter had never been so high.

"Wow ... What's that over there, Ronan?"

"The cemetery ..."

"Oh ..."

They rarely thought about death; death among them was an occasional event and usually, it was one of the older generation who, being less able, worked in the kitchen or laundry.

"Is that where they buried Marion's baby?"

"I guess so ... Come on ..."

By the time they reached the top of the twelfth level, the wind was much stronger and buffeting them so that they had to hold on to the ladders tightly.

"Three more to go, Peter!"

Despite their training regime, his breathing was becoming laboured as his chest tightened and he had a pain in his side. Ronan seemed not so badly affected.

"I thought I was fit!"

Ronan laughed and ploughed on.

He remembered why they were doing this and asked, "Can you see anything yet?"

"Not until we're right at the top ..."

He didn't bother to look over his shoulder, in any event, the sweat was running into his eyes.

At the foot of the last ladder, he pleaded to have a break.

"At the top, there's a wide platform and a kind of turret thing. At the top of the turret, there's a walkway all the way around the flagpole.

If you stand on the edge of the retaining wall and look towards the setting sun, you'll see it.

They both looked out. It was just possible to see over the wall now. He'd never seen anything outside the compound and even though the mountains in the distance were hazy, he could not but gaze in wonder. The smudgy silhouettes seemed unearthly compared to the shining white *plastocrete* all around him. They did not look dangerous, but altogether sad and lonely.

"Ready?"

"Yeah ..."

They scaled the last level. Just as Ronan had described, the top platform housed a kind of turret. The spiral staircase inside led them up to the flagpole. It was surrounded by a walkway, as wide as a man, hemmed in by a waist-height retaining wall.

Even without standing on the wall, they could almost see the base of the mountains, now cloaked in shadow as the sun moved to within a finger's width of the top-most peak.

"It's vast ... Our whole world is so small ..."

He looked in all directions. To the west were the mountains. To the east, a flat plain. To the South, nothing but sky as if the land dropped away sharply. To the north, a flattish plain that narrowed to a point where the mountains in the west appeared to meet a darker outcrop, which Ronan thought must be a forest.

"Trees ... I wonder if there are animals in the forest."

"I've never seen so much as a bird in the sky ..."

"How do we do this then?"

"Pretend to be cleaning the flagpole." Ronan handed him a cloth from out of his pocket. "Just be careful, Peter ..."

He used the pole to steady himself as he clambered on to the top of the wall, which was about as wide as his foot. He turned and hugged the pole. It took a minute for his eyes to adjust to the glare as the sun was now almost directly in his eyes. Hanging onto the pole with one hand and shielding his eyes with the other, he peered out, his line of sight angled just above the edge of the wall.

"What am I looking for, Ronan?"

"You should see something shiny – it's very narrow."

He wondered if the sun and the haze had tricked Ronan's eyes but just as he was about to give up, he saw a glint far off. He guessed, rightly, that the sun had to be at the perfect angle to hit the edge of the blade.

"I see it – just a glint, but I see it ..."

He clambered down, eyes bright and shining as if he'd seen some kind of miracle.

"I saw it, Ronan."

"That wasn't everything that I wanted to show you ... Look over there ..."

Ronan lifted his arm and pointed north but within the compound, "... see the base of the wall?"

"Yes, I see ... What am I looking for?"

"The waste pipes ..."

"I see them – what's different?"

"There is a new cable running alongside the waste pipe ..."

"Are you sure?"

"It wasn't there during last term ... It's new and I think it goes under the wall, but I haven't been out there to check ... We should get going or we'll raise suspicion."

Back at the base of the Hive, they parted company, a new pact forged between them.

"Sunday then?"

"Yes – meet here at ten o'clock to receive the grace from Manager. Thank you, Peter."

"Thanks, Ronan ..."

His mind whirred all the way home. He did not even notice Marion in her garden.

"Peter!"

He came to with a start.

"Marion! How are you?"

"Fine. Are you rested?"

"Yes; I'm fine now. I'll be back at the farm tomorrow."

"Good, because Toby has been a major jerk – I brought food for you. I didn't realise you were out with Ronan."

"Practice run before Sunday ..."

"Is it true what they say?"

"What do they say?"

"That you can see the ocean."

"I don't think so ... You can see the mountains and that's pretty much it."

He chatted for a few more minutes if for no other reason, to give the impression that everything was as it should be. Once they'd said goodnight, he hopped into the dome to sit down, unable to piece everything together, knowing there was something else that must explain everything if only he could fathom it. He racked his brains until his head hurt. He gave up and went to water the plants.

Manager stepped up to his gate, taking him by surprise.

"I just wanted to make sure you were okay, Peter."

"I'm fine, thank you."

"Good; I will be in tomorrow to re-arrange the space – we need to instal another row of tanks-"

"Why?"

"To increase production even more, Peter – and if this keeps up, we'll need to double the on-shift crew. Very good!"

He had wanted to ask why they needed to increase production even more – their numbers varied so little – a birth here, a death there. Of course, he knew why – thought he knew, "To feed more than just ourselves ... private communications ... a new wind turbine ... something brought in from the outside ... So, there's a settlement out there – why haven't they told us? Why would they not tell us that someone had survived?"

In his own mind, there was no reason. But it felt tenuous. He needed something more concrete, but he couldn't define exactly what apart from going outside and seeing it all for himself – and that still scared him even though he had seen over the wall.

To occupy his mind, he got a bucket of water and began to clean the windows outside, which were always so dusty.

The physical exhaustion was nothing like the mental fatigue. Once he'd cleaned the windows, and eaten something, he lay down, and his eyes closed the second his head hit the pillow.

He came to with a jolt and found himself bathed in sweat though he hadn't remembered dreaming at all. He was suddenly aware of the sound of someone's breathing.

"*Ali Ben?*"

"P-e-t-e-r ..."

"Yes ..."

He sat up and swung his legs over the side of the bed. Ali Ben was at his side before he'd levered himself to his feet. He slipped his arms around the man's waist and hugged tightly, pressing his cheek against the man's chest. The man cradled his head tenderly. He had no idea why he was looking to this man for answers to questions that he had not yet even formed in his head. He supposed it was just the contact he craved, especially when the guy kissed the top of his head. He couldn't remember the last time – no one remembered their mothers or fathers; there was no tenderness until they were paired up as he and Gwen had been.

Ali Ben moved away slightly, prompting Peter to look up into his eyes. He saw the man's smile and smiled back. With no foreplay, he felt the man's need rise between them. He had the overwhelming urge to suck on the thick stem. He pressed his lips to the imprint of the thick shaft that the *nyleen* did such a bad job at hiding. The thin material was soaked and stuck to his lips. Without thinking, he slipped his fingers over the edge of the waistband and pulled down. They slipped part of the way but snagged on the thick blunt head. He used his lips and teeth to liberate it in the end, already intoxicated, watching self-control disappear down into the void like water in the sink when the plug was removed.

He pulled Ali Ben in until the furry base of the shaft was pressed up against his lips. It wasn't that feeling he wanted but the sensation of the thick head sliding into his throat, making him have to concentrate on his breathing, all to trigger the fantasy of being tethered to this *tube* that nourished him. The man slipped his hands around the back of his neck and pulled in harder, bucking upwards, barely moving but clenching and expanding the head that then filled his throat before subsiding a little, allowing him to take a breath quickly. He hadn't ever wanted to be used so roughly – had never used David like it or allowed David to use him like it.

Ali Ben withdrew quickly and left him gasping, but before he caught his breath, the man was pushing him back and lifting his legs onto his shoulders so that he could probe, and as soon as he hit his mark, he plunged in. The shock coursed through Peter's body like a lightning bolt. All he could do was reach out, grab the majestic buttocks that were thrusting into him and ride the waves.

oOo

Three times Ali Ben had taken him. He would have taken any amount of punishment.

As they recovered, he limped to the alcove and found a piece of paper and a pencil. Ali Ben watched him intently. In what little light filtered in from the security lights, he drew a rough plan of the compound and the mountains far away and then passed both paper and pencil to the cleaner, who, at first, was unsure what he wanted him to do.

"Ali Ben – you – *miliki* – *kidani* ... where – *nda?*"

The penny dropped. The man picked up the pencil and drew a circle about halfway between the compound wall and the mountains.

Peter drew a rough sketch of a wind turbine. Ali Ben nodded furiously and smiled.

"*Isimu?*" Peter desperately wanted to know the name of the town if it had one.

"*Isimu? Midiji?* ..." and Ali Ben pointed at the circle and added, "... *Mbathwi* ... *Mbathwi.*"

As if they had reached a point of no return, both sat back from the table. The paper and the pencil lay before them; to Peter, it was more dangerous than a bomb ticking away.

Scared but still curious, Peter asked, "*Ona?*"

"*Tsi hale* ..." and Ali Ben drew five circles on his wrist.

Peter held up his hand, splaying his fingers, "*Usiku* – five *usiku?*"

"*Ewa* ..."

Ali Ben got up to leave, prompting Peter to get up. This was unknown territory. A snatched hour at changeover with David was all they had ever really managed. Writing in the diary and hours of silent communion beside his lover's pod made him realise that he was so ill-prepared for anything outside of the normal run of things.

Ali Ben drew two circles on his wrist and Peter just nodded. It wasn't until Ali Ben wrapped his arms around him and begged for a kiss that he found the strength to animate his limbs.

"Thank you ..."

Ali Ben left him standing in the centre of the room with his head held low.

Eventually, he crawled into bed and buried his face into the sheets to inhale the reek of sweat and sex.

Chapter Four – Founders' Day

It was easier to work through it and ignore everyone for the most part. When Marion asked him what was wrong, he gave the usual answer, the irrefutable one, "I'm just missing Gwen ..."

Over the course of the next two days, they were incredibly busy, installing additional equipment and readying the seedlings for planting into the new tanks.

Peter found it hard to fight off Marion's and Manager's enthusiasm, knowing that the extra produce would not be feeding the community. They finished late on the second day, earning themselves a rest day. Peter hung back after Marion had left, to retrieve the diary.

Skipping dinner again, which was becoming the norm, he ran to the dome and hid the diary with the medallion and the map. With nothing else to do, he visited David's pod. Being the furthest from the entrance, he ended up walking the entire length of the facility before arriving at the pod, which was identical to the others. Being that time of the day, he was alone, and recounted everything that had happened since changeover, ending with the only question he had for David, "What the fuck are you doing? If you had been caught, you would probably have been marshalled and we wouldn't have seen you again."

For the last quarter of an hour of his visit, he lay his head on the pod and tried to empty his mind of all the confusion. After paying Gwen a brief visit, he headed back home to wait for Ali Ben.

While waiting, he resolved that, if he ever decided to leave, he would only leave with David, and anyone else they chose to tell – he found it hard to imagine that Toby would not choose to leave with them. He was less sure of Ronan. He had no idea how the girls would react. The only other thing he agreed with himself was to investigate the tunnel but only after he had seen what happened on Founders' Day. It had not escaped his mind that Ali Ben was leaving on the same day, and presumably, the fete was in part designed to camouflage their departure and the arrival of the fresh crew. Only then did he realise how little attention he had ever paid them – he was sure, even now, that Ali Ben was the only one whom he would recognise again.

It was very late by the time that Ali Ben arrived. They hugged and kissed for a full fifteen minutes before Peter invited him to sit down and drink some water. He went to ask a question, but Ali Ben pressed his finger to his lips and shook his head. After which he got up and held out his hand. Sensing this was the last time they would probably see each other, he let Ali Ben tow him to the bed, except, instead of taking him roughly as he had before, he rolled over and pushed down the back of his shorts.

He stripped quickly, deafened by the thumping of his heart in his ears. For a full five minutes, he lay on top of Ali Ben just trying to catch his breath. Once calmer, he rose up on his arms, peeling himself away from the hot, sweat-slick skin of the man he had come to in some way, if not love, then cherish. Ali Ben repositioned himself, raising his buttocks fractionally, and in so doing, grazing Peter's sack. It was what, seemingly, had been lacking because he suddenly got very hard. Never having had the chance to really savour the moment, he probed carefully and deliberately before settling so that the head of his cock was just resting on the tight little rosette of perfectly pleated folds of skin. Ali Ben's groan quickened his pulse, and he drove in, smoothly and silently until his bush was pressed up against the man's hole. He lowered himself, sliding his hands in under the man's chest, hugging tighter and tighter until Ali Ben complained, and then he began to thrust hard, pounding for everything he was worth.

oOo

Nothing was said. They simply sat, looking at each other, smiling, Peter especially, who had *performed* twice before Ali Ben had taken him again and again as if their lives had depended on it.

Would he see him again? Maybe he thought, maybe on the outside. Until the last changeover, leaving had never been contemplated. There had been no reason to think that there was anything to leave for, and no reason to think that anything would ever change. Now, some cold hard facts made him question just what they were doing, what they had been told, what was truth and what was a lie. The idea of leaving was no less terrifying, but he no longer shied away from thinking about it.

One of the security lights stuttered; it made them refocus. Ali Ben got up.

"*Lala unono*, Peter ..."

"*Lala unono*, Ali Ben ..."

They hugged for an eternity until Ali Ben just slipped away, leaving Peter sobbing quietly. Rather than crawl into bed, he dragged one of the chairs outside and sat on the little patio, listening intently to every noise that broke the silence – the hum of the lights, the ever-present thrumming of the generators, the faint whirr of the fans drawing air up into the Hive to keep it cool, the far-off drone of the water pumps, and the occasional cry of a child, waking up from a nightmare. Only when the lights clicked off, did he move back inside to prepare for the day, which was a study day.

After grabbing an early breakfast, he donned his running shoes and started to jog out towards the circuit path. Pacing himself, he arrived at the drain cover just about when he figured most everyone else would be at breakfast or just leaving to go to the library. He bent over as if he had a stitch in his side and peered into the gloomy interior of the box. He could just make out the shiny prongs of the digging fork.

"How the hell did you even know this was here?"

He bent down on one knee, pretending to tie his laces, and inched closer to the edge. After a quick glance, he put his hand on the cover and gave it a shove; it was surprisingly light, and he dislodged it without even trying.

"Fuck; here goes ..."

He slid the cover away and sat on the edge, readying himself to drop in. After another glance over both shoulders, he pushed off and let himself fall. The drop was about six feet. He landed on something soft. While he waited for his eyes to adjust, he dropped to his knees to feel the bottom; it was sandy with some grit mixed in. As the gloom lifted, he could make out the digging fork, which was propped up against the pile of material that, he assumed, David had already excavated. The outline of the fairly squat tunnel entrance was clearer now. When he probed the tunnel, he found the material was more compacted, but it still broke away fairly easily. After fifteen minutes of digging with just his hands, he was already another foot deeper, but the pile of material behind him was building up.

He took a breather to assess what to do. He spread out and trampled down the loose material with his feet, wondering how far in the tunnel was blocked.

"Just a bit more ..."

He picked up the fork and crouched in the opening to the tunnel. Using the fork, he worked some more of the worst compacted stuff loose. Large chunks fell away. He cleared as much of it to the back of the box as he could, piling it up so that he had enough space to work but also to provide a step to make getting out easier. After half an hour, he had dug out a few more feet. He had a ledge knee-high at the back of the box, which he'd compacted as much as he could. Figuring he'd been gone from the dome for about an hour, he bargained with himself to dig for ten more minutes before clearing up. He thrust forward and as high he could, given the height and the slope of the roof.

Clang

"Shit!"

Whatever he'd hit had sent a nasty shockwave up his arm; pain flared in his wrist, which had taken the brunt of the blow.

Dropping the fork, he massaged his arm and wrist. A lump of the material fell forward, burying his feet. Though it was dark, he could see the surface was different – smoother and brighter.

"What the hell?"

Using his hands to dig, more material fell away, revealing more of the surface. He investigated further, finding the edge of what he assumed was a door. It felt cold to the touch. Instinctively, he felt for a handle or lock. He found some kind of mechanism, two bars, running across the centre of the door; the ends of the rods slotted into the frame, effectively locking it. At the centre, where the bars met, a series of toothed cogs held the rods in place. He found a wheel right in the centre, which he assumed when turned, operated the toothed gears, drawing back the bars and unlocking the door. The wheel was locked solid and would not budge.

"I need some oil ..."

He shuffled back out of the tunnel and turned, stretching himself to his full height. The far-off sound of voices made his heart skip a beat. Knowing that, if anyone ran past the drain, they would see the cover had been removed, he had no choice but to risk sliding it back if he could and wait it out. Stepping up on the ledge that he'd made, he craned his neck to look over the lip of the box. With his eyes full of sweat and grit, he could just make out the tiny forms of two runners. He had less than ten seconds to slide the cover back or risk being seen.

With his heart pounding and holding his breath, he stood up, reached out, congratulating himself for not moving the cover too far away. He dragged it back and then crouched down in the shadow, hoping the runners would be too engrossed to notice anything.

As the voices drew nearer, he could make out the distinctive voices of the two Techs who ran the water treatment plant.

"Come on, Joel – keep up the pace!"

He knew that was Sirus; he'd often watched them train together; they were the fittest of the guys he saw around the campus. Thankfully, the heat, the dust and the sweat drove them on with, allegedly, a promise of a shower at the end if what he heard Sirius say was right.

He waited for a good fifteen minutes. Fearing others might also be out on the track after a period in the library, he hid the fork in the tunnel, and eased himself out of the hole, keeping as low a profile as he could. He re-fitted the grate and kicked the sand and sharp-edged stones about to mask his footprints as best he could. He stepped up on the track and started to jog but the knowledge of what he had done and the growing realisation that maybe David was right, drove him to pick up the pace, buoyed up on a kind of euphoria. He made it back to the Dome just in time to avoid Marion, who was coming back from the library. He showered quickly and then dragged his seat outside. When Marion re-emerged, he was sitting and reading.

"Where were you?"

"Hey, Marion ... I went early," and he brandished his book to make the point, "and then I went for a run ..."

"You missed breakfast again ..."

"I had some crackers ... Want to go to the botanical enclosure?"

"Oh ... Uhm; sure. Whenever you're ready."

"Give me ten minutes ..."

He slipped back inside to finish towelling off and to put on clean socks and his normal shoes.

oOo

"Ronan was asking after you; that guy gives me the creeps sometimes."

"Leave him alone; he's okay ... He probably just wanted to confirm tomorrow's schedule ... What books did you check out?"

"Time management! I don't know *how* we're meant to get it all done."

"Manager said that he'd double the crew."

"Yeah, but who's free?"

"True ... I really don't know why we're producing so much more food; there aren't any more of us, are there?"

His question was a deliberate attempt to sound out Marion's thoughts.

"I suppose it can be frozen and stored in case there is ever a problem with supply ..."

He hadn't thought of that.

"That would make sense ... I don't see any other reason."

"I for one don't mind being busy because the time goes quickly but standards also have to be maintained."

It was true that they kept everything scrupulously clean, everything was recorded, and everything was always double if not triple checked.

"I forgot to say that I cleaned David's pod last night."

"It's fine; Tech told me you were in – thank you. We'll do them together after our visit, shall we?"

"Sure."

"Why did you want to go to the botanicals today?"

"I-I haven't been for ages ... I thought it would be a nice change."

They wound around the compound to a secluded area that they as farmers had access to without needing a slip. The dome was climate controlled and housed, they were told, as many *old-world* species that could be saved.

Peter loved the cactus plants and the epiphytes, in particular, the orchids.

They entered the outer reception, signed in, and then donned a head-to-toe suit to stop any contaminants getting inside the sphere. Once they had passed through the airlock, they fanned out to find their favourite specimens. Though it had a been an off the cuff suggestion, Peter was very happy Marion had agreed to come. The multitude of plants, arranged in tiers, created a quiet oasis. Water was delivered by ultra-fine sprays. All the plants were grown in a nutrient-loaded gel or, as in the case of the cacti, a bleached grit-like substrate.

The wandered around for at least an hour before they caught up with one another.

"This was such a good idea, Peter ... This always reminds me of the film of the children walking through the woods ... I know I have never seen a wood, let alone walked through one, but I would love to, wouldn't you?"

"I'd rather swim in the sea, but a walk in the woods would be just as nice ... Do you think the outside will ever recover?"

"Outside? I don't know, Peter – not in our lifetimes ... I do sometimes wonder how we'd ever know if it had – I suppose we'd see birds and insects ..."

"Only the wall protects us; we breathe the same air as outside – I can't believe it isn't safe."

"Maybe you should ask Manager or Director ..."

He'd asked again to find out what Marion might be thinking – was it possible that so few – largely David, Ronan, and him – were curious?

"... The earth is scorched, Peter – how would anything start to re-grow?"

"We could seed it ..."

"You should ask ..."

They toured the facility for another hour before retreating back to the outer lobby to change and get ready to enter the Hive to clean.

It was lunchtime.

"I'll do it, Marion; don't miss lunch. If you see Ronan, tell him where I am."

"Missing another meal?"

"Crackers or gloop? I don't think I'm missing much."

"Fine. I'll see you later, yes?"

"Sure ..."

It wasn't that he didn't appreciate the offer of help to clean but he needed some time to think and that was always better achieved in the relative coolness and in the soothing, blue-bathed light of the Hive.

He headed for David's pod first. He wiped down, check vitals, recorded the numbers and changed the filters in the local air con unit. He said nothing out loud. He did the same at Gwen's pod, but then sat down and pressed his ear to the pod to listen to the artificial heartbeat. It was very calming as always.

The scrape of a boot made him jump; he turned and found Ronan walking towards him.

"Peter?"

"Do you have the pennant?"

"Yes; at my dome ... I was coming to check on Amy ... I saw you go off running this morning; was it a good session?"

"Y-yes; pretty good. Marion and I have just been to the collection."

"Yeah, she said ... Mess hall is closed tonight so the tables can be set up for the feast tomorrow – do you want to eat together at home?"

"S-sure; why not? Come to mine ..."

"Will you invite Marion?"

"I don't know – should I?"

"I'd prefer it if you didn't – she always acts weird around me ... See you later then."

With which, Ronan trundled off, leaving Peter somewhat perplexed. Disagreements rarely existed, let alone surfaced – there was nothing worth arguing about. Tensions like this made everyone feel uneasy – it usually spread like a fungus and was really hard to eradicate. Unfortunately, Ronan had been at the centre of most complaints for the last ten years. He'd seen enough diary entries from David to know what Gwen thought about him.

He put his head back down and mulled over the idea of talking to Manager about cultivating plants outside the wall – he really couldn't see why they hadn't already tried.

He agreed that he would talk to Ronan about it first. He was beginning to think that the only reason they didn't, was to stop them from seeing something.

On his way back, he sneaked into the farm and took a small bottle of the oil that they used for lubricating the wheels of the overhead lifting equipment that was employed in moving the heavy tanks.

Just as he got back to his dome, Marion spied him and came outside to invite him to dine with her.

"I've invited Ronan to dine with me; I assumed you'd be with the girls."

"That's okay, Peter ... Just don't get tarred with the same brush ..."

He side-stepped the comment, which he thought unjustified. Crackers and water seemed like poor fare to offer any guest, so he hopped to the kitchen and grabbed some gloop and some of the crisp *spiro* sheets that they were trialling.

After cleaning and setting up, it was approaching dinner time. In hiding the oil, he found the medallion and his mind instantly flew to Ali Ben, who would be leaving the following day. His chest tightened. It made him think about why he liked him beyond the obvious physical attraction, which there was, but then he'd always been attracted to the type – hairier, thicker-set, and freer in their movements and attitudes. David was taller than average, had wide hips and a perter behind than most but he had none of the same charisma, or was it machismo? He couldn't decide. All he knew was that he was going to miss the man more than he cared to admit to himself.

He changed into shorts and a vest top because the air was warming with the season, and the winds had swung and were now blowing up from the hotter south. When Ronan arrived, he was dressed as always, in his long pants and a long-sleeved shirt, buttoned up to the neck with the sleeves rolled down and buttoned tightly around his wrists.

"Hey, Ronan ..."

"Is Marion coming?"

"No; she's with the girls ... Water?"

"Thanks ... You're not angry with me, are you; for inviting myself?"

"Why would I be?"

"Most people don't want to talk to me – even Toby just jokes around ... You talk to me, but I know what they say and maybe they'll say the same things about you, especially if you don't eat in the mess hall."

"I don't care what anyone thinks, and I'll eat what and where I like ... Speaking of which, I got the new crisps to try. Dig in!"

Strangely, he liked Ronan more and more, largely, he thought because he wasn't always joking around.

"Tomorrow will be great; I love Founders' Day, don't you?"

"I guess so ... Does it really mean anything more than an ice cream these days though?"

"Without them, this wouldn't be here, and neither would we ... so we have a lot to thank them for ... That's how I see it."

"I agree, but it was so long ago ... Don't you think we need to move on somehow?"

"How?"

"If you're right, if what we saw was *truly* a wind turbine that means there are others – outside ... Why are we avoiding them?"

"But only you and I have seen the blade ..."

Did he mention the medallion? Before he could decide, he thought of the most obvious question he hadn't yet asked, "Why haven't you told Manager?"

"He'll think I'm crazy and I'm already taking enough medication."

"But he could climb up and see it for himself, couldn't he?"

"But if they're hiding it from us, and I tell them that I've seen it, it might not be so good for me ..."

"Or me ..."

He saw no reason to tell anyone anything ... yet. Not until he had seen what happened on Sunday, knowing Ali Ben was leaving. If Ali Ben left, he knew the rest must be true – and then he would decide what to do. He still couldn't decide if he should tell Ronan about the tunnel.

"You went running again today ..."

"I went early before study period started ... Climbing up to the top of the Hive proved how unfit I was."

"I like to run but not by myself ... David always told me to get lost whenever he went out ..."

"You're more than welcome to come with me next time ..."

It seemed easier to side-step the issue until after Sunday.

"These new crisps are not bad ..."

It signalled a lightening of the mood and conversation for which Peter was more than grateful. They played some games, mainly noughts and crosses and hangman, and spent an hour weeding and watering the garden. The noisy exodus of the girls from Marion and David's pod made them take stock.

"It's getting late, Ronan – what time are we meeting tomorrow?"

"Meet at breakfast ... I don't have to go just yet ... not unless you want to get an early night."

"No; I'm fine ... Gwen left some books if you want to read something ..."

"Maybe I'll just sit quietly ... if you don't mind."

"Not at all ..."

He busied himself with clearing up and finding clean clothes for the following day, which necessitated cleaning his shoes. Throughout which, Ronan stayed seated at the dining table and meditated, or so it seemed to Peter.

"Ronan ..."

The man came to, and stretched, yawning widely.

"Sorry; I think I dozed off there for a time ..."

"It's fine; it's time for bed ..."

Ronan got up, replacing the chair precisely under the table before taking his glass to the sink.

"Goodnight, Peter."

"Night, Ronan ..."

Once Ronan had left the pod, he started to get ready for bed, washing his face and cleaning his teeth. With the rising temperatures, it was more comfortable to sleep naked. He slipped off his shorts and vest, relishing the relative coolness.

There came a knock at the door.

"Who is it?" he cried out, grabbing the vest to cover his groin.

"Ronan; I forgot my medication pot ..."

"Wait a second, Ronan ..."

Whether Ronan had heard him or not, the door opened, and Ronan walked in, "Sorry, Peter – oh, shit! I'm so sorry. I'll come back-"

"Ronan; chill for goodness sake. You've seen me naked before. Find your pot."

But for both of their sakes, he slipped his shorts back on while Ronan checked the bathroom for his medication pot.

"I knew I had left it on the shelf – I daren't not take them."

Peter turned, seeking out Ronan's face to give him his much-needed reassurance. He saw Ronan's eyes drop to his groin, and rest there just a little too long, and it was enough to make his cock buck; a fact not lost on either of the men.

"I-I should get going, Peter ... b-busy day tomorrow ..." but Ronan's eyes dropped again, and Peter was powerless to rein in the all-too-common reaction. When Ronan licked his lips, something snapped.

"Ronan?"

"S-ssorry ... I-I just-"

Whatever he might have planned to say was squashed under Peter's lips. When Peter broke off, Ronan raised his hand and Peter assumed it was to push him away but when Ronan touched his cheek, he moved straight back in, this time the pressure was returned, and then Ronan's hand snaked around his neck and pulled him in tightly.

oOo

He couldn't mask the fact that his hands were shaking but he was determined to undo the buttons of Ronan's shirt himself, looking forward to the moment when the thin fabric slipped from the man's shoulders and exposed his scrawny chest.

With an uncustomary display of confidence, Ronan left his hands resting on Peter's waist. Ronan watched Peter's hands, and only when the last button was undone did he look up into Peter's eyes, which smiled back at him, encouraging him to slide his hands under the waistband of his shorts and grip his proud mounds.

"So hard ..."

"Nothing like yours ..."

"I climb ladders all day; I s-suppose that helps ..."

The comment hung in the air as Peter pushed the shirt off of his shoulders, letting it fall to pool at Ronan's feet. When he reached for the zipper of Ronan's trousers, Ronan stuttered a plea, "D-don't tell anyone, will you."

"Of course not ..."

"I begged Amy not to tell anyone that we've never done it, but I know she told Denise – goodness knows who else knows."

"Don't worry; I won't tell anyone ... You've never done it?"

"N-no ... Can you show me what to do?"

He'd never heard a voice so full of pain and unexpressed need before.

"It's okay; we'll take it slow ... I promise I won't do anything you don't like."

This seemed to pacify Ronan; enough to allow Peter to unzip and unbutton his trousers so that, swiftly thereafter, Ronan was standing naked before him. He slipped off his own shorts to be naked too. It was Ronan who moved forward so that their cocks were touching.

Assuming he would need to take the lead, Peter asked, "What do you want to do?"

Ronan didn't reply but dipped his head to kiss the side of Peter's neck. Encouragingly, he reached around and clasped Ronan's buttocks, pulling in, squashing their up-turned cocks between their stomachs. Lifting his head just a little, Ronan dipped lower and kissed his throat, before sliding down, peppering his chest with kisses.

"You smell so good, Peter ... like ... like the old books with the pressed flowers between their pages ... you know the books I mean?"

"Y-yes ... Ronan, fuck man ... Suck me!"

With little or no precursor, and before he could take his next breath, Ronan had sunk to his knees and was gripping his shaft. "*Please*, Ronan ..."

Before the words had died, Ronan engulfed him, and it was all he could do to stop his knees from sagging beneath him. When Ronan sucked, he clenched and instinctively reached for the man's head to support and guide him. It took all his self-restraint to stop himself from thrusting into the willing throat. And willing it was because Ronan took more and more of his length until he felt the man's throat close around his cock. There was no holding back then; he thrust, simultaneously clenching, and with each inward thrust, he raised himself a little on his toes and found something extra to give.

The surge was swift and powerful but also painful. The pressure in his sack made him grit his teeth; it seemed only to add fuel to the fire that licked at the soles of his feet, the softer skin of his inner thigh, the small of his back, his delicate rosette-like nipples and along the entire length of his cock. When release came, it sent hammer blows into his guts.

"Ronan!"

oOo

He didn't know how he got there but when he became aware of the room, he found himself on the bed with Ronan's head lying on his chest and his arms loosely draped around his neck.

"Ronan ..."

"Mmmm ..."

"What happened?"

"I think you forgot to breathe ..."

"Unreal ... How are you doing?"

"I'm fine. It's just so good to hold you ..."

It did feel good too. He and David never had the chance.

In the next few minutes, as he regrouped, he felt the tell-tale twitches that signalled that he was not yet done, and he hoped Ronan wasn't ready to go. He twisted his torso to bring his head closer to Ronan's. He kissed his brow, receiving a satisfied murmur.

"You were amazing ..."

"I never thought it would be like that ..."

"Do you want to do anything else?"

"I'm not sure ... Do you?"

"I'd like to suck you too ..."

He heard the whirrings inside Ronan's head and hoped he'd get the chance. The man's prick was thick and topped off by a fat head, which he could only guess at how good it would taste.

"Okay ..." the voice didn't waiver but betrayed a nervousness understandably.

Striking while the iron was hot, Peter slipped down to nuzzle and nibble at the soft skin of Ronan's sack, which was already tightening as his prick swelled and lengthened, revealing a beautifully smooth head. He savoured every second and every square millimetre of the soft, furry orbs that were unshaven and covered in a blond down. The arching cock grew out of a nest of darker scrolls, already beginning to gather into spikier quills as their sweat began to run freely. Intoxicated on the man's musty scent, he licked the shaft, taking his time, never having the opportunity, sometimes gathering loose skin between his lips, and pulling gently, sometimes nibbling the flattening edge of the retracting foreskin, sometimes flicking his tongue across the slit that dissected the perfect mushroom-heart-shaped crown that glowed pink like a sunset. Licking his lips, he prepared to engulf the flaming brand.

"I may not last, Peter ..."

He stole a glance and smiled wickedly as he opened his mouth and ate the head, sucking in his cheeks and closing his lips tight around the shaft just beneath the now engorged glans. Almost immediately, Ronan threw his torso back in rapture, arching his back and driving the stalk inches higher and deeper into the greedy and willing mouth.

oOo

"Stay; why risk being seen?"

It was kind of obvious that he should stay. It was already very late.

"I suppose it makes sense; I don't want to get caught by Marshal – If I slip out at dawn, no one will be the wiser ..."

Peter pulled him back into the bed and wrapped his arms around him and kissed his pert little nipples. Any reticence or nerves had long gone. They were comfortable with their bodies and sharing everything that was offered. After Peter had sucked Ronan to a climax, he was ready to plough his arse and did so. Ronan had fucked him back and then they had fallen into a deep sleep for a few hours. Revived a little, thirsts sated, it was time to explore without the same desperate urgency. Sensing nothing was out of bounds, Peter turned Ronan over, and buried his face between the globes of his behind, licking up the sweat and the traces of his seed, teasing the bruised and swollen edges of the tiny rosette, raking Ronan's back with his fingertips to cause him to clench and pump out more of the seed. Expecting Ronan to be less comfortable, he was surprised when he returned the favour and more so when he gently fingered him and slowly fucked him, until his whole body spasmed. Their communion ended with another satisfying mutual wank into each other's mouth.

oOo

"I'll meet you at the mess hall; after breakfast, we'll collect the pennant and get ready to climb, okay?"

"Yes; Manager will give us grace and then we start the climb while everyone watches. Once the pennant is hoisted and unfurled, the cheer goes up and our job is done."

"How long do we wait before we climb back down?"

"Not long – fifteen minutes until the crowd has dispersed and everyone has gone inside to join in the feast."

"Okay. You'd better go ... I don't have the words, Ronan."

"None are needed – it was so much more than I could ever have hoped for."

"I'll talk to you later, okay?"

"Yes; okay ..."

Ronan left the pod and scooted back to his own before the Tech crews changed over at the Hive, meaning the paths were deserted. They knew Marshal would be in the kitchen, grabbing breakfast.

Once his companion had left, he showered as thoroughly as he could, scrubbing himself until his skin was pink. He donned clean shorts for the time being, slipping on a pair of old shoes before stepping out to enjoy the relative coolness of the dawn, relishing how his skin seemed to tighten.

"You're up early!"

He swung round to find Marion watering her plants.

"Busy day; lots to do ..."

"I'll clean the pods today ... Please be careful up there; it looks terribly dangerous."

"It's not that bad really ... What's happening after the feast?"

"We're trying to get Manager to approve opening the swimming pool."

"Yes!"

"It's nice to see a smile back on your face – walk with me to breakfast?"

"Of course."

"I'll knock for you."

"Okay ..."

Often it was the simplest things that lifted everyone's spirits. By the time they were all assembled for breakfast, the rumour of the opening of the pool was rife and Manager's appearance at breakfast heightened speculation.

Nothing was said until after everyone had taken their plates and cups to the cleaning station and had returned to their seats.

"As of all of you know, today is a special day – Founders' Day. In a short while, Ronan and Peter will climb to the top of the Hive and hoist the pennant ..."

The boys found each other in the crowd and smiled broadly.

"... When the pennant has been hoisted, the feast will begin, and after that, I have approved the opening of the swimming pool for the rest of the day-"

What other things he had to say were lost in the almighty cheer that went up from everyone in the room.

Once the hubbub had died down, Manager gave grace,

>"... *Oculi omnium in te sperant Domine:*
>*et tu das escam illorum in tempore opportuno.*
>*Aperis tu manum tuam,*
>*et imples omne animal benediction ...*"

No one understood the words, but the delivery ensured that no one spoke, and everyone held their breath for the duration. A special kind of peace descended on the room, and spontaneously, everyone reached out and held someone else's hand.

>"... *Benedic, Domine, nos et dona tua,*
>*quae de largitate tua sumus sumpturi,*
>*et concede, ut illis salubriter nutriti*
>*tibi debitum obsequium praestare valeamus,*
>*per Christum Dominum nostrum ...*"

Manager then clapped his hands and led everyone outside. Ronan had delivered the pennant in it's carrying case to the Manager before breakfast, he now ceremoniously gave it back the boys, and Peter shouldered it. They set off to loud and enthusiastic applause and cheers, which carried them up the first flights.

Unlike before, they kept the pace slower and did not take a break at any of the platforms. It was tougher going but they ignored the burning pain in their muscles as everyone watched their progress.

When they reached the last platform, from which the turret rose, Ronan unpacked the bag and rolled the pennant up and thrust it under his arm for the last stage.

At the top of the turret, they threaded the rope through the eyelets and hoisted the pennant to the top of the flagpole, watching with bated breath as it unfurled and began to flap in the brisk breeze.

The cheer went up.

The men hugged each other, laughing and crying at the same time.

Without trying to draw attention to himself, Peter circled the turret's walkway and looked out for any signs of movement. He kicked himself for not thinking to sneak into the disinfectant store that morning and spy on the yard to see who was coming and going.

"How would they get them out?"

He'd run around the entire perimeter of the compound; there was no gate in the wall. He'd found – David had found – the tunnel so there could be another but where?

How could they move an entire crew out and a fresh one in without drawing attention to it ... unless there was a diversion.

"The pool!"

"Peter?"

"Sorry; the pool is going to be open today; I'm so happy!"

"I didn't think you could swim ..."

They waited for the crowd to disperse, signalling that the feast was about to start.

"Shall we go down, Peter?"

"Yeah; I just love it up here ..."

He could see nothing out of the ordinary. Everyone was where they were meant to be. Ali Ben had told him he was leaving so something was going to happen. Staying longer would raise suspicions. He followed Ronan, picked up the bag and began the long climb down, begging Ronan for a break as before. The lower they got, the less he could see.

Back on the ground, Ronan took the bag back to Manager's office and Peter headed into the feast, being corralled by some of the lads, who patted his back, and then by the girls, with Marion had their head, who congratulated him.

"You did it! Well done. I'm so proud of you."

"Don't forget to thank Ronan too, Marion."

"If you say ... Get something to eat and then we can go home and get changed for the pool."

Caught up in the general revelry, he didn't see Ronan come in, who everyone ignored. He picked up a plate of food and took it over to him.

"I wanted to thank you for allowing me to help you today; I really appreciate it, Ronan."

"It wasn't anything really to do with me but for what it's worth, I was proud you did it with me – it does mean something, you know – not to most people but it does to me."

"I know ... I wish Amy could have seen you; she'd have been proud of you."

"It's not easy for her ... On next changeover, we're going to ask to be separated so that she has a chance to have a baby ..."

"Seriously?"

"Yes – but don't tell anyone yet, please ... She deserves to be happy."

"But what about you?"

"I'm happy to do the things I get told to do – and I'm happy that you are my friend ... I could teach you to swim?"

"Uhm; I guess so ... I can't believe what you just said."

A *reassignment* was rare – Peter couldn't remember the last time it had happened apart from when Keith had died, and Marie was left alone. She'd been reassigned to the kindergarten so it sort of worked out. There had never been a voluntary separation in the whole of the last ten years.

"We talked about it last time ... It's fine; better for both of us. She'll have a baby and I won't have the pressure anymore ... Let's get ready for the pool party, yeah?"

"Sure; I'll meet you there ..."

Walking back to the dome, he was bombarded with thoughts, chiefly, the impermanence of everything when, on the face of it at least, nothing changed inside the compound. Then he realised that so much had already changed – even in the last two weeks. He'd found the medallion and had met Ali Ben, he'd found the tunnel, he'd climbed the Hive and seen the turbine; he'd spent the night with Ronan.

"What does it all mean?"

He didn't know what it meant but he knew something was going to change. After the party, there might be a chance to go back to the tunnel and try and loosen the wheel, he figured.

He put all thoughts to one side, hoping to enjoy the party. Despite his best efforts, he could not completely put Ali Ben out of his mind.

"We'll see what happens, won't we ...?"

He changed into trunks and grabbed a towel, slipping on his poolside shoes, and jogged off, determined not to miss out on the rare treat. If the pool party was intended to be the diversion, he still had no idea where the exit was, and it could be that they had already moved under the cover of darkness.

The troubling thoughts began to dissipate when he heard the screams and splashing, and the kindergarten had been allowed to play too so there were kids everywhere, all of them demanding to be picked up. In the end, it was a riot, and he hadn't seen everyone enjoying themselves as much since the last pool party – including Ronan, who was teaching some older kids to dive.

Much of the day was spent playing in the water, ferrying food and drinks from the mess hall, organising games, and chatting to everyone until Director showed up and announced the film for the evening.

By late afternoon, people were beginning to drift away. The kids had gone back to school. Manager announced that the film would start in an hour. Peter was one of the last to leave, having taken Ronan up on his offer once the pool had quietened down. As they towelled off and got ready to walk back to the domes, he noticed out of the corner of his eye, a cleaning crew mustering to start the job of cleaning down the pool area. He stole a glance, but he recognised none of the men, all of whom were eyeing him and Ronan up, barely disguising their lust, unashamedly sporting wood that was barely concealed by their thin *nyleen* shorts.

He and Ronan wandered off, first dropping back their trays, and then heading for the domes.

"Great day, wasn't it?"

"It was fantastic, Ronan ... I'm gonna shower – probably see you for the film, yeah?"

"You bet!"

He toyed with the idea, abandoning the tunnel, but as work started the following day as usual, his opportunities would be limited. Maybe if he showed his face and then dived early, he mused.

Marion's call decided for him. She was in higher spirits than of late.

"I can't remember the last time I had so much fun ... Hurry; we don't want to be stuck at the back!"

He felt his chances slipping away but there was also a part of him that wanted to forget all about it and go back to being completely ignorant of the facts.

They joined the rest of the filmgoers and watched, for the hundredth time, the story of the two children lost in the woods. When they happened upon the windmill, he found tears in his eyes despite his best efforts.

"Softy!"

"Shut up, Marion. It's the dust."

"Of course, it is. I'm going to the library after this. I'll see you tomorrow at the farm."

"Yes, okay."

Everyone, including Toby and Ronan, seemed to be off to do things. He scurried back to the dome to change. He hid the oil container in his little carryall along with his water bottle and towel, and headed off.

Once he'd arrived at the drain, he quickly opened it up and dropped in, remembering to replace the cover. Nothing had been disturbed. It took fifteen minutes to clear enough of the material out from around the base of the mechanism to get to the cog that operated the locking bars. He doused it in oil, reserving some for the barrels of the heavy-weight hinges, and sat back. He wasn't even sure that he wanted to open it, and even if he did, he wasn't convinced he'd go on alone.

When his rump started to go numb from sitting on the stony ground, he got up to check the wheel. There was some give, and the bars shifted a fraction. He kept turning the wheel one way and then the other. The grating sound put his teeth on edge. He used up the rest of the oil. For a while, nothing seemed to want to give, and then a jolt shifted the wheel a full quarter turn and the bars slid back but still not enough to be free of the slots in the frame.

"C'mon!"

Wondering why he hadn't thought of it before, he used the shaft of the digging fork as a lever and jammed it between two of the wheel's spokes and strained as much he dared to avoid breaking the handle.

It moved by shuddering degrees until the bars were free of the slots, at which point, the door shifted slightly, and a blast of cold air rushed in from around the frame.

"Finally!"

"What was that!?"

The sound of the voice made him freeze. He didn't recognise it. Seconds later, someone else said, "Don't tell me you believe in ghosts!"

It was Manager's voice.

"Fuck!"

"Don't joke about it! I *definitely* heard something – take a look ..."

He knew there was probably no more than a minute before he was discovered. He couldn't imagine the trouble he'd be in if he were to be caught.

Screwing up his eyes, praying the hinges did not squeal, he pushed on the door with all his strength. Above him, he heard Manager say, "I can't see anything; it's too dark. Anyway, this is the one we need to get the crew to clean up after the north side is sealed."

The door was incredibly heavy, and it barely moved; slowly but surely, it swung back. The cool air chilled the sweat on his face and chest and the torrent running down his back.

He strained his ears for the sound of the grate being moved.

"Get the crew down here tomorrow – C'mon! We need to sort the delivery ..."

"I swear I heard something!"

"You imagined it. Let's go!"

He waited on the threshold, poised until his muscles screamed with cramp. It had grown dark outside. He was in near pitch-black himself now. The little bit of remaining light did nothing more than highlight the edge of the door and the gulf beyond.

Inch by agonising inch, he moved back until he was clear of the door, which he pulled shut. With the last of his strength, he closed it and turned the wheel to lock it. Sitting back on his haunches, he breathed deeply and waited for his heart to stop pounding.

He readied himself to leave, wondering if he shouldn't take the fork back, knowing that, if the crew came down, they would find it and questions would be asked.

Agreeing with himself that he had to, he eased the grate back and popped the fork out first. He clambered out, keeping low. Once he'd replaced the grate, and scuffed up the entrance to hide his tracks, he ran as fast as he could all the way back to the dome, praying that Marshal was somewhere else. At the dome, he threw the fork in the long grass and slipped inside, panting hard but so relieved that he felt sick.

"Where the fuck have you been?"

Chapter Five – High Stakes

"I swear, Ronan; that's everything I know ..."

The silence that followed became increasingly heavy, unbearably so.

"... I don't know what to do ..."

Still Ronan said nothing.

"... Ronan!"

When his heart had stopped hammering after the shock of finding Ronan seated at the dining table, he had told him everything. Ronan hadn't said a word throughout.

"I-I don't know what to think ..."

Peter fetched the medallion as a way of distracting himself. He placed it on the table in front of Ronan, who still didn't move.

"... There's a town or a village out there; the cleaning crews live there – Ali Ben came from there – the medallion proves it ... There are deliveries to be made – You and I both heard him say it; you showed me the new conduit ... David found the tunnel and I found the door. There is a way out ..."

"Everything is a lie ... Everything we've been told is a lie."

"I don't know what is a lie or what is the truth, but I do know that there is something out there and, for whatever reason, we've been kept in the dark ..."

"Why?"

"I don't know but I think we have to find out ..."

"Who do we trust?"

"I have no idea who we can trust – not Manager, not Director – but we *have* to trust each other."

Before anything else was said, Ronan rushed from the table and leapt to the bathroom to throw up.

oOo

"Stay ..."

"Is it safe?"

"You're safer here with me than by yourself ..."

"I'm sorry."

"Don't be silly; it's too much to process ... Just try and relax, maybe get some sleep. We'll decide what to do tomorrow."

More tired than he could ever remember, Peter quickly used the bathroom and flopped onto the bed naked, leaving Ronan seated at the table, recovering, sipping some water.

Soon afterwards, he turned, trying to find a comfortable position to ease the aching muscles in his back and shoulders, and almost instantly, his eyes closed where he was welcomed by a gulf of nothingness.

Thinking it was still part of the dream, it was only when the tightness around him relaxed somewhat that he realised he was semi-awake, and Ronan was spooning with him. He felt the shuddering breaths as they fanned his back, assuming that he'd finally found some sanctuary of his own. He pushed back and wrapped Ronan's arms more securely around himself before diving into the abyss again, welcoming the cloak because, as much as anything else, it hid David's questioning eyes from view.

But sleep never did quite come to him completely. He tottered on the edge of the void, grateful for the fact that he didn't have to try and make sense of the landscape of thoughts, still conscious of the thin body wrapped around him, and the enormous prong that slotted so neatly into the cleft of his buttocks. Maybe it was that alone, he mused, that kept him from sinking into a deeper sleep. He was comfortably swollen, by no means hard, and happy not to be plagued with the urge to touch himself.

When he felt a pair of cool lips pressed to his cheek, he realised that he must have dropped off at some point. When he began to turn to seek out those lips, he felt the scrawny arms attempt to push him onto his stomach. He smiled to himself as he rolled onto his front.

Those same lips peppered his back with feather-light kisses, from his neck all the way down to the deep narrow V at the top of his cleft. He reached back with both hands to stroke the thighs that were astride him and gripping him so tightly. The sensation of skin beneath his fingertips filled him with a need.

"Ron-"

"Shush ... I got this ..."

There was nothing to do but abandon himself to the tender ministrations – the kisses, caresses, nibbles, licks, and strokes, each of which heightened his senses, giving the air a keener edge. Before it became intolerable, Ronan shuffled up and planted his cock within the cleft, thrusting gently to massage the blooming rosette that lay within, causing Peter's spine to corkscrew and the hairs to go up along his forearms. His nipples and his sack tingled with heightening arousal as the rock-hard stem found less and less resistance and sunk deeper inside his gut.

"R-o-n-a-n ..."

"Quiet ... I want this to last and last ..."

The lengthening strokes, that became progressively harder and quicker, made him concentrate on his breathing to stop himself from clenching. It was addictive to allow the experience to grab hold and take him over. Every in-bound thrust blossomed in his gut; every withdrawal, left him craving the next stroke. Grabbing fistfuls of the sheets and biting down on the edge of the pillow, he suffered the exquisite torment and laid himself bare, relinquishing control and abandoning himself to the roiling boil of his blood, sweat and tears until Ronan climaxed ecstatically, and within seconds, the scrawny collection of limbs tumbled beside him as Ronan collapsed.

Only when he moved did he then realise that he'd cum too. Euphorically and light-headed, he reached out and dragged Ronan into his arms to seek out his mouth for a lengthy kiss.

"I love you ..."

oOo

"What are we going to do?"

Dawn was turning the eastern skies pink. An hour remained before they had to leave but before then they agreed a plan was needed.

"We can't risk raising suspicion, Ronan – we still need to know more – like about the deliveries, and how the other crew got moved out. I can use the excuse that I need more oil to go to Maintenance and maybe pick something up there. What excuse could you have to go to the north side?"

"None usually; there's only the cemetery out there ..."

"Damn ... Maybe we'll have to go after dark ... He definitely said *after the north side is sealed* – does he mean a tunnel?"

"I don't know but it sounds a lot like it ... But why seal it?"

"Who knows ... Did you mean what you said?"

He'd hadn't responded at the time because he didn't know how to – didn't want to rush out an answer in the heat of the moment only to regret it the second the words left his mouth.

"When I said *I love you*? Yes, I meant it."

"Do you know what it means?"

He thought he did. He thought he loved David, but he doubted it now. He'd never loved Gwen – not in that way. He knew the difference between love and lust – he'd lusted after Ali Ben but that was all. They'd been encouraged to love their partners since their pairing, being told that they would grow to love each other more with every passing day. He missed Gwen's enthusiasm and chatter and her knack of knowing, on changeover, when to leave him be and when to suggest that they cut short dinner and head for their dome. So often, he felt that everyone else knew him better than he knew himself.

"I know that I wouldn't risk getting caught for anyone else ... Is that the same?"

He had to agree that it probably was the same.

"I think it is the same – I don't know how I feel, Ronan. I *do* know that I would never want anything to harm you ..."

"It's enough for now ... We need to go. I'll try and get out to the north side. You go to Maintenance. Please be careful."

"You too ... We'll meet later, okay?"

"Yes, okay ..."

Ronan left first; fifteen minutes later, Peter trooped out and headed for the farm. It was easy to manufacture a reason to go to Maintenance and he left for the workshop after all the checks had been done.

"Get some new bulbs as well, would you, Peter?"

"Sure ..."

It was easy to manufacture a reason to go but hard to keep his mind from whirring. Maintenance was on the other side of the yard to the Disinfectant Store. When he arrived, the yard was empty. While he waited for the Tech to find the right bulbs for him, he stood outside in the sunshine and watched. He could hear voices from behind the gate to the cleaners' compound, but it was hard to decipher anything. There was no window on their yard from the back of Maintenance. He wished he had another reason to go to the Disinfectant Store.

As luck would have it, just before the Tech called him back in, the gate opened, and the crew stepped out. He stole a glance, keeping his eyes lowered; no one was wearing a bandage, he noticed. He tried to etch a few of the faces into his mind. As he turned to go back inside the store, he heard a low murmur followed by a chuckle and assumed it was something lewd being shared between some of the men. He wondered if Ali Ben had said something on the changeover – how easy he was. But he somehow doubted it because the man had appeared to be decent and caring.

"These are all the new bulbs we have, Peter; Manager requisitioned extra for the new row of tanks, but I can't get them. Go easy."

The comment did not really register until he got back to the farm, where he found Manager. He relayed the fact.

"Can't get them! What are they doing in there?!"

Both he and Marion backed off, having never seen Manager angry before. It took a minute or two before he calmed down.

"I'm sorry; they were requisitioned weeks ago ... This is very frustrating and completely avoidable ... Carry on; I need to speak to Director ..."

They said nothing for a few minutes.

"Why are these tanks so important, Marion?"

"I heard a rumour ..."

His ears pricked up, "What?"

"I heard that if we grow more food, it might be possible to close the Hive down and let everyone be together for more of the year ..."

"Who said that?"

"One of the girls overheard one of the Tech guys ..."

"Why haven't we all been told?"

"I guess until these tanks are operational, nothing is going to happen ..."

It was a sobering thought. Their whole lives were dominated by the Hive and the six-month changeovers. A world where they were all together was hard to comprehend.

"Best we go easy on bulbs then ... Wow ..."

"It's just a rumour, Peter ..."

He wondered if Ronan had heard anything. He became impatient to see him, but it was barely mid-morning. He hadn't found out anything else as useful at Maintenance; he hoped Ronan had found a way to go to the north side.

They convened at lunchtime when Marion melted away to join the girls and he was left to sit alone – or so he thought before Ronan walked in and made a beeline.

"Hey ..."

"Talk later-"

"Did you go?"

"Later ..."

"I heard a rumour ..." and he recounted what Marion had said.

"We know that is probably not true – it'll be a cover story."

"Manager will have to say something if the rumour is out – he'll know what people are saying."

Almost on cue, just after Toby had entered the mess hall, Manager made an appearance.

"Okay; settle down. I'm aware of a rumour circulating about the Hive – I can tell you all right now that the rumour is not true. The reason we are trying to grow more food is to create a surplus to put into storage so that, if we ever lose a crop, we won't starve. *That* is the reason. Believe me, if there was *any* way we could all be together, you would be the first to know ... Thank you."

No one spoke until after he had left the hall. Toby piped up and asked, "Why would the Tech say it if it wasn't true?"

No one had an answer and an uncomfortable silence settled on the room. Only an announcement fifteen minutes later that informed them that the pool would be open again for after-work recreation did the mood change. Peter looked into Ronan's eyes and the truth was plain to see.

"He's lying ..."

oOo

A chance to play in the pool was not to be turned down lightly. Everyone went, including Peter and Ronan. Without the kindergarten, there was more space and Peter practised his strokes.

"You said later – what happened this morning?"

"Not here ..."

Before they left the pool, he searched out Marion to ask her what she thought.

"It's what I said to begin with – I didn't believe the rumour."

He doubted that but found it more interesting that she chose to distance herself from it – maybe *she* had overheard the Tech herself and she had been the source of the gossip, he mused.

He jogged home to shower and change, heading back to the Hive to clean, rendezvousing with Ronan as arranged, on the upper level by David's pod.

"So?"

"I saw the crew come back while I was washing the upper floor windows – that's all I saw."

"We have to check!"

"If it's sealed, there won't be anything to see – better to check the other one to see if they cleaned out the pit ... Don't you want to see what's beyond the door?"

He did, it was true. But he was afraid to look in case it confirmed everything – if there was a world outside, what possible reason could there be for denying it?

"You're right, and I do ... But we'll need a torch."

"Leave that to me ... I'll come by later ..."

With which, Ronan disappeared, leaving him to contemplate the fact that he was keeping yet another secret from the diary.

oOo

"Where did you get it from?"

"There are torches throughout the Hive in case of power failure. They keep spares in my cleaning cupboard. Let's go ..."

He'd packed water, a towel, and a handful of crackers. They both wore their running kit to put Marshal off the scent, who was snooping around the domes. He ignored them.

By the time they approached the drain, Peter could see that things were different. The area had been swept clean for one thing. Huge bags of the material he'd found in the pit and piled up against the door were lined up neatly along the side of the path. The grate was propped open and a ladder had been installed.

"Why?"

"I don't know, Peter ... Are we going down?"

"I don't think we have a choice – we have to know ..."

He went first, borrowing the torch, which he only needed once he'd reached the foot of the ladder. There again, everything was swept clean. He waited for Ronan before proceeding into the tunnel. The torchlight was reflected back, confirming that the door too had been cleaned. Something caught his eye. At his last visit, it had been too dark to see much detail. He'd mostly found his way by touch. High up on the top edge of the door was a little plaque, riveted in place. The little metal cartouche was no bigger than a seed tray label; it was incredibly hard to read.

"I don't believe it ..."

"What is it, Peter?"

"You remember the medallion and the name on the back?"

"*Noble Scholar?*"

"Yeah ... except it isn't his name ... It's the same name that's engraved here ..."

"What does it mean?"

"Whoever made the medallion, also made this door ... That's what it means."

"Are we still going on?"

They had come this far, he debated; there was no reason not to open the door – and all the signs were that the answers to their questions lay beyond it.

"Yeah ..."

The wheel turned smoothly, and the bars slid back noiselessly. The door opened an inch, and the same cool draught buffeted their faces.

Peter turned just before pushing the door back, "Sure?"

"Yes ..."

He pushed and the door swung back on its newly greased hinges. He stepped over the low threshold and into the tunnel proper.

oOo

Though it was hard because the walls curved sharply, they squatted side by side and surveyed the tunnel.

"What could it have been used for?"

"Water drainage?"

"But it never rains ..."

"Not these days ..."

"Are you saying that this was not built by the Founders?"

"I think that is pretty clear now ..."

"What now?"

Even with the benefit of the torch, they could not see the end. It was too dark for any light to filter in from the other end, they judged.

"Come on ..."

Peter led, having to stoop to avoid hitting his head on the ceiling. They made rapid progress until they came to the top of a sharp incline.

"I think we've just passed under the wall."

"The ground must slope away steeply, you think?"

"Yes – when we looked south from the top of the mast, we couldn't see anything beyond the wall because the land drops off ... If we climb down, I don't think we can get back up ..."

"Damn!"

The incline was at least fifty feet long and made from the same smooth material as the rest of the tunnel.

"We're gonna need a rope ... Where the hell does this lead?"

"I don't know, Peter ... but why clean it up?"

"I think if we knew that, we'd know a whole lot more ... What do we do?"

"Come back with a rope?"

"I guess we have no choice ..."

As they turned, the noise of a dull thud made them freeze in their tracks.

"Fuck!" Ronan growled in a hoarse whisper.

"We need to shut the door ..."

He scuttled like a beetle along the short stretch of tunnel to the door, which was, thankfully, half-closed already. Shielding the light from the torch, he couldn't see into the outer chamber. Something had been thrown into the pit. He closed the door but, in finding no locking mechanism on his side, all he could do was hold it fast, praying no one wanted to come through. Closing the door cut off all sound. Ronan joined him and pressed himself up close.

"Who the fuck is there?"

"I don't know but I'm sure we don't want to be found ... Let's just wait ..."

Minutes ticked by. It started to get very cold. The torch was already starting to dim.

"Peter-"

"Okay ... Stay behind me ..."

Steeling himself, he took a few deep breaths and pulled the door open. The heat struck them both. It was a relief for their tired and cramped muscles. Peter trained the torch into the pit around the foot of the ladder. Three or four large lumps were piled up on the floor. They appeared to be bags of some kind – the kind they used to bag up the discarded *spiro* that had spoiled in the drying frames.

They inched forward.

"What are they?"

"I don't know; I'm guessing rubbish ... None of this makes sense."

He reached out and prodded the nearest bag with the torch; it was firm and yet yielded a little, but it didn't move much. The neck of the bag was tied tightly with a cord.

"Hold the torch, Ronan; I'll untie it."

He handed over the torch, which Ronan trained on the neck of the bag.

It took at least a minute to loosen the knot; when it came free, the neck of the bag opened and peeled back slightly.

"Rags? It's full of rags ..."

"That doesn't make any sense at all," with which, Ronan pulled the neck of the bag, and then wished he hadn't.

"Oh no ... no-no-no-"

"We've gotta get out of here!"

Peter was first to grab hold the ladder. He sprang up the first few rungs and then reached up to push the grate open, which had been closed by whoever had tossed the bags into the pit. He met resistance.

"Peter; get moving!"

"I can't open it; it's locked ..."

oOo

"They're all members of the old crew, aren't they?"

"Yeah; looks like it ... Now we know why we didn't see anyone leave ..."

They'd opened each bag, only to find that each one contained the body of one of the cleaners. He'd prayed and prayed that he wouldn't find Ali Ben among them. That prayer, at least, had been answered.

"What the fuck do we do now?" Ronan asked just as the torch started to flicker. He turned it off to save the battery.

"If they find us, we're dead like them ... We have to get back in and tell everyone."

"How do we get back in?"

"If they're shipping the *spiro* out of the compound, there has to be a way."

"You mean go outside and find a way back in ..."

"Yeah ... And we have about twelve hours to do it because if we don't show up for work tomorrow, they'll search the pod, find the medallion, and start to add two and two together ..."

"Shit ..."

"We have no choice ..."

Fortunately, they'd brought their water, and while they slaked their thirsts, they sat and held each other's hand.

"What if we can't get out of the tunnel, Peter?"

"Then we'll come back here and wait for someone to come by – and take whatever chance we have ..."

"Okay ... Shall we go then?"

"Yeah; it'll be slow going because the torch is gonna give up pretty soon. We don't need much light thankfully. Let's go!"

Buoyed on adrenaline alone, they scurried back through the door, which they left open to give themselves a little bit more light, and pretty soon, they found themselves back at the top of the incline.

"This is it. We'll never climb back up ..."

"I'll go first-"

"No, Ronan; I'll go ... If there's no way out at least one of us has a chance-"

"We'll go together ..."

Was that what love was?

"... Whatever happens, we stand a better chance if we're together ..."

"Okay ..."

Bracing themselves as best they could, using the rubber soles of their shoes as brakes, they slid down the incline. Their assessment was accurate because halfway down, the incline became that bit steeper. Towards the end, they lost control and slid helter-skelter fashion on their backsides until they tumbled out onto a wide ledge, beyond which there appeared to be nothing. Sweeping the ground with their hands, the torch, having now failed, they found the edge of the platform and some kind of balustrade. Levering themselves back onto their feet, it took a few minutes for the vast space to take on any form.

"Oh, shit ..."

"What the fuck is this place?"

Peter knew he'd seen something like it before. He racked his brains.

"I know what this is ... It's a turbine hall – there's a picture of one in our history book."

"But ... but that was tiny ..."

"Yeah ... actually, it was just a scale model ... This is the real thing ..."

They both looked over the edge of the platform, steadying themselves against the balustrade. Sure enough, hundreds of feet beneath them were the massive, silent, motionless blades of a huge turbine.

Chapter Six – Tinder Box

Some light was filtering in from somewhere; the gloom lifted enough to show them that the platform upon which they had tumbled, nearly surround the entire hall. Directly opposite their untidy point of entry, they could just make out what looked like another tunnel. They jogged around the gallery and found a narrower tunnel.

"Looks like an overflow, Ronan ... But where did the water originally come from?"

"You know what I think ... I think the compound used to be a huge reservoir, feeding the turbine ..."

"Could very well be ... Let's see where this leads ..."

It was a tight fit, and they proceeded in single file. Peter went first, feeling his way along the smooth floor, which tilted slightly but not anything like as much as the main inlet. Fifty paces into the tunnel, he found a grid, blocking their path, but it was clear that just further on, the tunnel opened to the outside.

"Damn ..."

"Is it solid? Can you move it?"

He grabbed hold with both hands and pushed and pulled for all he was worth. There was some movement; investigation showed that many of the spars were rusting. Lying on his back, using his feet, he kicked out at the weakest spots until he was exhausted when Ronan took over. Eventually, some of the spars snapped and the whole grid began to move more and more. Some of the stonework fell away and more spars snapped. It finally gave way when they put their shoulders to it. It fell and clattered on the tunnel's floor. They pulled it back along the shaft and dumped it on the wide platform. It gave them more space. Inching forward, they found the very edge of the tunnel and pushed their heads and shoulders out, instinctively looking down. A silvery ribbon, a long way beneath them, glinted in the moonlight.

"A river?"

"I think so ... running out to the sea – we were right about this side dropping off. The craned their necks to see to the West and in the direction of the mountains. The bluff curved, blocking most of their view; they fantasized that they could see a few twinkling lights, but it was more likely the moon reflected in a couple of lakes, they agreed. Ronan, more used to climbing, eased himself out and clambered onto the top of the tunnel's mouth, finding that the tunnel was surrounded by some stone or brickwork, that formed a decent ledge above the opening. The very edge of the bluff was about twenty feet above their heads.

"Can we climb up, Ronan?"

"There are some decent hand and footholds, especially at the sides where there are some metal rungs, but I'm not sure if they'll bear our weight ... I guess there's only one way to find out-"

"Be careful, Ronan."

"We have to try ... We don't have time to climb all the way down ..."

Inching along the ledge to the upright part of the brickwork surround, he found the first of the rungs, which he assumed had been used to access the tunnel for maintenance. He tested the first and it didn't budge. He knew that when he stepped off the ledge and trusted the rungs, there was no guarantee one of them wouldn't fail. Peter knew it too, but they had already agreed there was no time – and no other way out.

"Wait 'til I get to the top, Peter ..."

He knew the reason. If Ronan fell, and he was beneath him, he'd knock him off the wall too.

Was that love, he mused – making the sacrifice?

Through experience, and maybe desperation, and fuelled by adrenaline, he clambered to the top of the ladder, and threw himself on the hard ground at the edge of the bluff.

"It's fine, Peter – come up ..."

He was less experienced but no less desperate and just as pumped. With his eyes closed, he put his trust in the metal rungs and clambered up. At the top, where he reached out, expecting to find another rung, but finding nothing, he panicked. Ronan's hand grabbed his arm.

"I gotcha ya!"

He climbed the last two rungs, and Ronan hauled him over the lip onto the edge.

"We made it," but the tone was one of relief – or more accurately disbelief - rather than one of celebration.

They rolled further away from the edge and caught their breath. When, ten minutes later, they stood up and turned to put their backs to the edge, they saw the wall of the compound loom up before them, half a kilometre away.

"Now we just have to figure how to get back in ..."

Peter chuckled, and soon they were doubled up with laughter; it was a necessary release of tension.

Before they moved on, they drank the rest of the water. Only by keeping moving could they avoid the chill of the wind blowing in from the south, in which they rightly detected the strong tang of salt. They scampered over the rough ground towards the wall, over what they assumed was the roof of the turbine hall. When they reached the wall, strangely, they felt safer.

"What are we looking for, Peter? Another tunnel exit?"

"The crews come in, and the *spiro* leaves, somehow ... Let's just follow the wall around to the west ..."

Progress was swift because the ground, nearest the wall, was barren and relatively even. It was warmer too and a relief to their sore muscles. Soon the curve of the wall receded, enough to reveal the deep purple outline of the distant mountains.

"We'll have to move up to the edge if we want to see the town, Peter ..."

Dare they spare the time? But he knew he had to see the town with his own eyes.

"We have to see it ..."

There was no disagreement. They angled their path away from the wall so that they would come to the edge of the bluff due west of the wall, in theory, directly opposite the wind turbine they had seen from the top of the Hive.

As they moved further away from the wall and closer to the edge of the bluff, the wind increased, and the temperature steadily dropped. By moving they kept warm but as neither had eaten for hours and they had no water, they began to slow down with fatigue.

"It must be three times as far to the edge from here."

"No fall away ... Soon, we should see something ..."

Peter hoped he was right; it all too easily felt like a wild goose chase or worse, an un-waking nightmare.

Progress was swift; the foothills of the mountains started to emerge as they approached the edge. Then Ronan grabbed Peter's arm and stopped them in their tracks.

"What it is, Ronan?"

"Look ..."

Not one but maybe fifty wind turbines emerged from the gloom. The one they thought they could see from the top of the Hive was to the right of the main group and slightly elevated.

It spurred them on to run the remaining two hundred metres, but the edge wasn't like the bluff's to the south. There was a gentle fall away, skirting the western side and much of what they could see of the north too. Way down, to the left of the turbines and in the middle of a dark patch, which they worked out must be trees, they saw the same three lights they'd seen from the bluff.

"Got to be the town, don't you think?"

"Definitely ... So; it's real – what now, Peter?"

Was that the meaning of life, he mused? Teetering on the brink of the next choice, never sure if it was the *right* thing to do, endlessly debating if he shouldn't just crawl back inside his safe shell. Was that why David had finally snapped?

"We have to tell everyone …"

"They'll never believe us …"

"Some will … But first, we have to get back inside …"

They skirted the wall to the north side, to the point dead opposite the south tunnel, as far as they could judge. The entrance to the north tunnel, if there was one, was not close to the wall.

"They said it was sealed anyway, Peter – but there *has* to be a way in …"

Exhausted, Peter threw himself on the ground; exhausted and frustrated, aware that time was running out.

"… The new conduit runs north, right?"

"Yes … A new tunnel?"

"The only place on the north side is the cemetery – no one goes there …"

He propped himself up on one arm and gazed at the wall; the wall that had defined his world for the last twenty-six years. Everything he had known was within the wall – everything until now.

"… If there is a way, it would be here where no one goes and no one can see anything … Peter!"

"I know, I know – let's start looking …"

The sky was just beginning to lighten in the east – the days were getting longer as they always did just after this changeover. Black turned to purplish-blue as they scanned the ground, which gave no real clues because it was stony just like everywhere else.

"You'd think there would at least be a track or a footprint …"

He sensed the panic begin to rise. He didn't know what would happen if they didn't show up for work – it had never happened unless someone was sick and usually a neighbour would knock and check and that would be that.

"... I don't even know what we're looking for, Ronan!"

"Just keep looking; don't panic ..."

He swallowed the lump in his throat and run his hand over his face to wipe the tears from his eyes. They worked out from the wall in a grid, scanning the ground, turning over larger rocks, moving further and further from the wall towards the scrub that lined the rough edge of the plateau. They swept the ground in an arc a hundred metres wide and came up with nothing. The purplish-blue was turning lighter by the minute.

"In the scrub, Peter; it's the perfect camouflage."

He had to wonder why they hadn't started there. The low bushes were covered in long, lethally sharp thorns. More than once, he got snagged or scratched. The little rivulets of blood ran down his arms and legs, but he didn't notice.

"Peter, come here!"

He staggered in Ronan's direction, "What?"

"Look ..."

He reached Ronan's side and looked down.

"The bush wasn't rooted; it came away in my hand ... Is that what I think it is?"

Set into the hard ground was a ring of metal. He bent down and started to clear the dirt away. An inch beneath the surface he felt something cold and smooth.

"Help me, Ronan; it's here!"

Pretty soon, they had uncovered what looked like a trapdoor. Most of the bushes were the same as the first; uprooted and just laid on the ground. By the time they had finished clearing away, they had revealed a door set into a frame, roughly two metres square.

"What's the betting it's locked?"

He had no hope that it was unlocked until Ronan grasped the ring and pulled. The door opened by an inch, but it was heavy, and he dropped it back down.

"We can do it together ..."

Ronan grabbed hold of the ring again and lifted it just enough so that Peter could get his fingers under the edge. "Please don't drop it ..."

He lifted with all he had left until the door rose by a foot, then Ronan dropped the ring and grabbed the edge. Together they managed to lift the door until it was open to shoulder height.

"I can hold it if I brace my arms, Ronan. Move round to the side and start pushing ..."

In that way, they managed to open it until it was pointing straight up. What was more remarkable than the door itself was the set of smooth, stone steps that led down from the edge.

"Push it all the way over, Ronan ..."

It teetered for a second and then fell. Fortunately, it landed on the bushes and didn't make too much noise.

"Come on; it's our only chance – Ronan; come on!"

He couldn't work out why Ronan wasn't moving.

"Ro-"

"Everything is going to change ... Those cleaners were dead; someone killed them ... There's a town down there – why are we going back?"

Why indeed, he thought for a second until he remembered the faces of the people that he had grown so accustomed to that if, for example, Marion dressed her hair even the slightest bit differently, he knew straight away, and if Toby said *dude* instead of *buddy*, he knew it was because he was feeling a degree less secure. He couldn't leave them in the dark.

"Because we owe everyone the truth ..."

Without waiting for an answer, he jumped down the steps two at a time. The east was turning a glorious pink and he knew they had one hour to get back.

As they guessed, the tunnel was new. It ran straight towards the wall. Further in, there were dim lights all along the edge of the roof on both sides. Stacked in places were boxes. He was tempted to stop and open one, but he knew that they contained *spiro* because every box was stamped G.L.O.O.P. in big red letters on the lid. There were other boxes too, but the letters didn't mean anything.

Fifteen minutes after entering the tunnel, they were at the foot of an identical set of steps, leading up to an identical door.

"We should have closed the other door, Peter."

"There's no time! Come on ..."

Together, they raised the door just enough to let them see outside. The low, retaining wall of the cemetery was just ahead.

"After three, okay?"

"Okay ... But what are we going to do, Peter?"

"Get back to the domes, clean up, report for work as usual ... Meet at lunchtime."

He said it, knowing they needed a minor miracle not to get caught in the wrong part of the compound.

"Okay; after three ..."

oOo

"Peter; you're late! I had to tell Manager that you were at the Hive."

"Sorry; I didn't sleep very well."

"You look like crap - He was in a foul mood because of the bulbs – like it's my fault!"

He let her vent for a few minutes, so pleased to be listening to her voice, which was so normal against the backdrop of all the weirdness and shocks of the last twelve hours. He and Ronan had parted at the head of the main path. Seconds after he closed the door of the dome, he heard Toby's whistle, knowing full well what he had been doing.

He had stood under the shower for a full fifteen minutes, scrubbing himself clean of the blood, sweat and dirt. He'd donned a long-sleeved shirt to hide the cuts.

"Why are you wearing a long-sleeved shirt? You're going to bake today."

"I didn't have time to go to the laundry yet ..."

"And another thing; Manager wants to ..."

He was grateful to Marion for sparing him the opportunity to think too much; he let her interminable drone just blot out the memory of the dead faces, staring back at him, almost pleading with him to do something. He'd crammed his mouth full of crackers and had glugged down a pitcher of water before leaving the dome but by mid-morning, he was feeling light-headed.

Marion noticed him fumbling with a tray.

"What's wrong?"

"Just hungry, I guess"

"You shouldn't skip so many meals or do so much running – it's not like we don't have enough food!"

"Marion! Enough!"

Something broke in that moment. The silence that followed her shock at his outburst hung in the air.

"Pe-"

"I'm sorry; I didn't mean to shout ... Marion; I have to tell you something ..."

The look on her face told him that she had absolutely no clue what he was about to say.

"... It's ... it's too big to cope with-"

"Are you sick?"

"No, no; nothing like that ... I can't tell you here – come to the pod later."

"Peter!"

"I'm sorry; I'll tell you later; just, just drop it for now – I'm sorry."

It was inevitable; he couldn't keep it hidden any more – he was surprised that he'd managed it so far.

"Go and get something to eat ..."

Her tone was almost maternal; he'd never heard it before. Before the tears sprang from his eyes, he scurried out and headed straight for the mess hall for a snack, also hoping to see Ronan and give him the heads up.

What he found made him glad he hadn't had anything to eat. Marshal was standing in front of Manager's office door, which was closed, barring all requests. Through the poorly drawn blind, he could see Ronan sat opposite Manager, whose head was bowed over something laying on his desk.

He feigned indifference, grabbed a snack, and scooted out, diving into the library to regroup his thoughts.

"Shit!"

Librarian found him in the horticulture aisle.

"Peter?"

"Oh, hey ... I forgot to bring back my books."

"Don't fret about it; bring them back at dinner time."

"Yes; okay ... D-do you have anything on irrigation?"

"Irrigation? Why?"

He grasped for anything to camouflage his rising panic, "I thought, seeing as we're trying to grow more crops that we could start planting up the waste ground by the wall ... Just an idea ..."

"That sounds like something you should discuss with Manager – it sounds like a very good idea *not* that I know anything about it ... There's something in the *Ancients'* aisle – bottom shelf ..."

"Thank you ..."

He measured out his steps to try and stop his heart from jumping out of his chest. When he found the book, he slumped against the shelving and closed his eyes, trying to breathe slowly. When he felt calmer, he checked out the book and strode back to the farm.

It was obvious that Marion had been thinking about what he was going to say when she asked, "Is it to do with Gwen? Are you planning to-"

"No; nothing to do with Gwen, Marion – please just wait."

"Okay; I heard a rumour about Ronan and Amy – I just wondered."

"What rumour?"

"They're splitting up."

"Who said?"

"I think Amy said something to Sarah at changeover – you know how Sarah can't keep anything to herself. Sarah said something cryptic, which sounds like she and Ronan are planning to separate – I can't honestly say that I blame her ..."

He let the rumour roll on; it spared him further interrogation until they parted company at four o'clock.

"Come to the dome later and I promise to tell you everything, okay?"

"Fine ... Just don't tell me you and Gwen are splitting up ..."

"We're not."

"Fine ..."

He held back, torn between rushing straight to the dome or finding Ronan.

Toby inadvertently helped him out when he rushed in, "Never guess!"

"What, Toby?"

"You've got to at least guess one time!"

"You've got someone pregnant."

"Hah! Who knows? ... Ronan's in deep shit ..."

His stomach flipped but he swallowed hard to stop himself from throwing up.

"What are you talking about?"

"... Found him snooping in the stores; stole a torch."

"What the hell did he need a torch for? Who told you?"

"That assistant Marshal – said he'd been put in the can ... Hurry up, man! There's gonna be an announcement ..."

He packed up quickly, throwing the light switch, hurrying to catch Toby up, who immediately changed the subject, "Where the fuck were you last night? I called in on my way to see Bethany ..."

"I-I went for a run."

"If you need exercise, just ask for a recommendation or three-"

"Toby!"

"Don't act shocked; you put on a good act, but I know you'd do it if you could just ditch your conscience for an hour ... You and Gwen haven't produced so something must be wrong ..."

"Nothing is wrong; it's just not our turn yet ..."

"Denise has shelled three ..."

"Are they all yours?"

"Dude! At last, some fucking humour! Of course, they are ... that girl is devoted to me."

"Pity you aren't devoted to her."

"I am!"

And he was shocked at the force of the reply. The two things didn't add up in his head. But as just as quickly, Toby passed it off with another joke, "I gotta make up for you slack heads! C'mon; we don't want to miss the announcement ..."

The mess hall was packed and there wasn't a spare seat. He and Toby were among the last to arrive, and they dived into two seats at the back. Manager was already standing at the front of the hall, looking, as far as Peter could see, ashen and clearly upset.

When he nodded at the back of the room, the doors were closed. Peter glanced around to see Marshal standing outside with his back to the doors.

"Settle down, please ... Settle down ... Thank you. We – the *community* – have but one rule ... we do not have secrets ..."

Peter nearly choked but stifled it, hoping he hadn't drawn attention to himself.

"... Secrets destroy our trust in each other and in the health of the *community* ... When someone breaks that trust, it is very serious ... Someone has broken that trust. It is hard to believe but it's true ..."

A murmur rippled through the room, emanating, as far as Peter could tell, from Marion, seated beside Bethany, three rows down.

"... It causes me great pain – *great pain* – to tell you that Ronan has broken that trust-"

"No!"

He couldn't be sure who had interrupted Manager, but he guessed it was Bethany – Amy's best friend.

"Quiet! Quiet please ... This is difficult enough ... Ronan was found stealing – this is especially serious because we have so little to spare ... For the time being, Ronan is being held in isolation for his own benefit. Everything will go on as before – you are not permitted to go near the block behind the pool. Anyone found trying to gain access to the block will be dealt with swiftly ... We will recover from this but only if we pull together. I am not asking for questions tonight. You will proceed as normal. A further statement will be made tomorrow. For tonight only, take your food home and do not leave your domes until breakfast – understood?"

No one spoke; everyone was rapidly processing the facts.

"Understood?"

"Yes, Manager!"

There were some notable absence voices from the collective reply – Peter hadn't replied and neither had Toby.

"Good. Collect your food and go home ..."

Manager disappeared quickly, leaving everyone stunned and stumbling about.

"Come to my dome tonight, Toby," Peter whispered behind his hand, adding, "I *have* to talk to you ..."

He received no reply except for a quick nod. Peter left him and sought out Marion.

"Grab some food and let's go."

Her face was a mess of tears and red blotches.

"I just know something bad is going to happen-"

"We have to go home and talk ..."

oOo

"Let's just wait for Toby, Marion ... Eat something ..."

"You're a fine one to talk ..."

Nothing else was said for the moment.

The food remained untouched.

Thirty minutes after they had left the mess hall, Toby slipped in through the door.

"This had better be worth it, Peter!"

He didn't take the bait; instead, he fetched the medallion, which he placed on the table between the two friends.

"What the hell is that?"

"That, Toby is the reason why Ronan is locked up."

"Can you tell us *what the fuck* is going on?!"

oOo

"... And we parted this morning at the domes ... I haven't spoken to him since – I saw him in the office, and you know the rest ..."

He had to give them their due; they hadn't interrupted once throughout the recounting of the events since changeover.

"Why the hell did he decide to take the torch back?"

"I don't know, Toby ... most likely, he thought it would be missed – or he simply decided to get it recharged."

"What are we going to do?"

He was fully expecting Marion to breakdown or tell him he was lying – not this calmness, almost steeliness.

"I don't know, Marion – I just hope and pray that he doesn't break down and say anything else."

"Yeah, because if he does, you're fucking history, pal."

"Yes, Toby ... and, unfortunately, everyone else if they think this has spread."

"They can't lock us all up, Peter; who would keep things going?"

"Don't be stupid, Marion; they'll slaughter us and open the Hive early ..."

Even Peter hadn't thought that far ahead.

"What are you saying, Toby?" queried Marion; her voice was quivering.

"What? It's obvious that's what they'd do rather than risk exposure ... We have to hope Ronan says nothing ..."

But they all knew, all too well, that under pressure, Ronan was liable to do anything.

Silence descended. It was so quiet, Peter could swear he could hear their heartbeats.

"What the fuck are we going to do?"

"I don't know, Toby – even if we spring him, what the hell are we meant to do with him?"

"Maybe he could escape and head to the town and bring help ..."

"We don't know who we can trust, Marion – he doesn't speak the language anyway."

"You do ..."

"I ... I know a few words ..."

"If they knew the cleaners had been killed, they might come ..."

"If I go, I'll be missed ..."

"No; it has to be Ronan because he's already outlawed ... But this isn't just about the cleaners; this is everything – it affects everyone."

"What are you saying, Toby; stage a riot?"

"If needs be ... That guy – *Ali Ben;* was that his name?"

"Yes; *Ali Ben* ..."

"He gave you the medallion – gave *you* the medallion – for a reason."

Peter thought he knew the reason and it wasn't to trigger an insurrection.

"Yes, he did ... But a riot, Toby?"

"We're living a lie, making all these sacrifices – for what?"

"How? How do you start a riot?"

Both of the boys looked at Marion because her tone brokered no negotiation.

"Before we do anything, we have to spring Ronan and get him to safety because, apart from you, no one else has seen the bodies or the tunnels ..."

"How do we spring him? The block is probably guarded by Marshal and the assistants-"

"They think he stole a torch, Marion; I figure there's just one assistant there for now – that changes if he cracks so we have to act fast ..."

"How?"

"We need a diversion ... What's gonna get everyone panicked, especially Manager and Director and the rest of those bastards?"

"Toby!"

"What? We eat *gloop* every day, work our butts off, bow and fucking scrape, say *thank you* for a dollop of shitty ice cream and have to spend every fucking day looking at the Hive!"

"A fire? A fire near the Hive ..."

It was Marion and Toby's turn to look at Peter.

"A fire?"

"A fire ... in the library-"

"No!"

"Makes sense, Marion. It's close to the Hive and, let's be honest, full of paper ..."

"Not the books ..."

Peter understood; maybe the only other person, apart from David and Gwen, who would understand but he knew nothing except a serious threat to the Hive would trigger the panic they needed.

"This is what we're going to do ..."

An hour later, Marion was the first to get up to leave, being the nearest and least likely to be spotted.

"I'll prepare as much as I can for him – do you honestly think that he'll be prepared to go?"

"He'll go; he knows it has to be him ... Take the dictionary and the medallion now. Bring the bag to the farm tomorrow. We've got oil at the farm. Toby gets a light stick from R&D and brings it at break time ... At lunchtime, Toby takes the bag to the laundry, I'll start the fire, and join him there. When the siren goes up, Toby and I'll go to the pen and spring Ronan, and you go to the muster point with everyone else, telling everyone you saw us at the laundry. Are we all agreed?"

"And we send Ronan on his way ... then what?"

"We have to hope that he comes back – the cleaners must have families; they surely will muster and demand to know what has happened ..."

They agreed it was the best chance they had.

Marion slipped out and they watched from the window as she dived behind her door without incident.

"I don't understand one thing, Peter."

"What?"

"Why did Ali Ben give you the medallion? He obviously thought you would be the one to stage this – he must have known what was happening ... maybe not for the first time."

"I think he gave *me* the medallion because I'd helped him when he got injured – there was a connection ..."

"He was right because I don't see anyone else having the balls to do this – and no one else cares about Ronan as much as you do."

"Which is pretty sad in itself ..."

"Yeah; things needed to change without this ... What was it like; outside?"

He didn't have to think too hard; he could still feel the wind on his skin and the pain in his eyes in having to capture the vastness of the space outside the wall.

"Wonderful, truly wonderful – it's vast, and ... and it's like everything you imagined it to be but a hundred times better."

oOo

The tension tasted like over-cooked *spiro* – bitter and indigestible. When he arrived at the farm, Marion was already there. She nodded in the direction of the little cupboard where they kept the spare filters for the air-con units.

They worked in silence, occasionally catching each other's eye, attempting to smile, invariably producing something more like a grimace. Both kept their eye on the clock. As the minutes vanished, the tension ratcheted up a notch. He could hear her thoughts; they matched his own.

"What the fuck are we doing?"

But it was all too easy to recall Ronan's face, his scrawny chest, and his vulnerability – above all that.

He made up tubes; it was repetitive and gave his head some peace. So much so that when Toby arrived, he didn't immediately guess the reason.

"Peter!"

"S-sorry ... I was – it doesn't matter. Do you have it?"

"Yes ..."

Toby handed over the light stick, used in the lab to ignite the gas burners.

"Just press the button a few times ... I'll come here and pick up the bag and go to the laundry at lunchtime; okay?"

"Yes ... Marion will go to the mess hall and I will go to the library. Wait for me. As soon as the siren sounds, we're on the move."

"Just tell me we have to do this."

"We *have* to do this, Toby – if for no one else then the families waiting back in the town for the cleaners to come back ..."

"Okay ..."

Toby left and, after checking the bag with Marion, to which, in addition to the dictionary, the medallion, crackers, and water, they added some of the dried *spiro*, another bottle of water and the note which he'd written the night before, which said, as best as he could manage - 'please help us; the cleaners are dead', they went back to making tubes and loading racks.

It felt surreal.

Manager did not make an appearance – they were not surprised but nevertheless still relieved. At a quarter to twelve, they stopped and just stood still, holding hands, quelling each other's jitters, and in Peter's case, wondering if this were a dream and he would wake up and find it was the day before changeover – when expectations were always highest, the thought of seeing David's face as thrilling a thing as he could imagine, and the anticipation of sharing more than just words, making his mouth water and his cock as hard as *plastocrete*.

In the silence, they heard the hands of the clock click and the faint sound of the lunchtime bell.

"Here goes then ..."

"Don't do anything stupid – if we have to abandon the plan, we'll think of something else."

"If burning down the library wasn't the stupidest idea that I have ever had ... I'll find you; don't panic."

He picked up his library books. He checked his pocket for the light stick and the little bottle of oil and walked out with Marion like he had done most days of their lives.

oOo

"Oh, Peter; can you just leave them there for me to check back in later – I have to go to the archive to find something?"

"Yes, of course ... Can I look for something on lichen and its uses as a soil improver?"

"By all means; just close the door behind you, will you?"

"Sure ..."

He waited by the counter for five minutes just in case someone else came by to drop off books. He then moved to the farthest aisle, bizarrely the one that had all the treaties and manifestos that they studied in History. He had to smile to himself when he saw, pinned to the wall at the end of the aisle, just like on every other wall, a copy of the *Community Constitution*.

He grabbed it, rolling it up, planning to use it as a fire starter, but first, he dragged out some of the smaller books and ripped out the pages from the heavy, leather covers, which he didn't imagine would burn so easily.

Once he had enough of the pages torn and screwed up in a pile on the floor by the edge of the shelving, he doused them with some of the oil, and then stood back. Using the rolled-up proclamation as a starter, he ignited the end, and when he had a good flame, he placed it carefully in the middle of the pile of tinder. Once he saw a trail of smoke and a flicker of flame, he doused the rest of the shelf in oil and headed back to the main corridor.

He was tempted to grab the book that had the dried flowers stuck to the pages but thought better of it. He slipped out and flicked the catch so that the door locked behind him. On the stairs, he met two young lads.

"Library is closed, lads. Come back later."

His age and seniority stifled any objections, and they scampered out, leaving him to ponder all the wasted years toiling away for what?

"To feed someone else while we survive on next to nothing – how could we be so stupid!"

Without looking back, he quit the building and headed straight for the laundry.

Chapter Seven – Ashes to ashes

He found Toby outside the laundry. The look on Toby's face telegraphed his question.

"It's done ... Let's hope it's enough. You've got the bag; let's go ..." Skirting the laundry, they scuttled along the wall that ran the full length of the pool until they reached the corner of one of the two changing blocks, which formed the entrance to the complex. They ran along the block's façade and dived into the shadows. From there, they had a decent view of the block in which Ronan was being held. It looked deserted.

"How long?"

"Not much longer ..."

"And once we've sprung him?"

"We go to the tunnel by the cemetery and let him out ... Fuck knows what happens after that."

"They'll know the fire was started deliberately – who saw you?"

"Librarian and two kids ... Once Ronan is on his way, it doesn't matter."

He knew that meant that he was pinning all their hopes on Ronan and his ability to get to the town, convince them he wasn't a raving lunatic, and get back with help.

The only other time the siren had sounded had been about five years before, to warn them of the storm that had hit without much warning. The lightning had damaged the generator, and for weeks, they'd had to manually crank the motor to keep the Hive supplied with electricity.

The ear-splitting sound shattered the silence. The protocol drilled into them since birth was to do whatever they were told to do to protect the Hive. The muster point was the yard outside the mess hall.

Thirty seconds after the siren had sounded, the door of the security block swung open and two assistants emerged, running full pelt.

"Two?"

"C'mon!"

"Wait, Toby ..."

He held onto his friend's arm, knowing there was no going back – the point of no return had already been reached, he admitted, when he'd lit the touchpaper. Once the assistant Marshals had disappeared from view, they proceeded cautiously. Once they'd crossed the space between the blocks, Peter inched towards the door while Toby ran around to the window on the blindside.

Taking a deep breath, he grabbed the handle and pulled it open just enough to slip inside. It was fairly dark; the blinds were drawn. A low, muffled moan alerted him to the presence of someone – he assumed Ronan. He couldn't immediately locate the light switch and used the light stick instead. It cast weird shadows. There was a door straight ahead. He launched himself at it, adrenaline pumping. Fear was replaced by a kind of abandon as if lighting the fire had done so much more than just send flames and smoke up into the air.

He didn't even bother to check if the door was locked; barrelling straight into it shoulder first, it repelled him for a split second and then the frame literally exploded, and the door crashed down. He stumbled, fighting to check his speed. His toe caught the edge of the door and sent him sprawling.

Recovering as quickly as he could, he leapt to the window to rip down the blind. Catching sight of Toby, he flung it open. Turning, he wasn't prepared for what he saw.

oOo

"Gently, Toby; I think his arm is broken ..."

Supporting him as best they could, they shuffled out of the room and into the outer space. He had to swallow hard and imagine he was moving something else, *anything* else just not the broken and bloodied wreck he had found tied to the chair in the corner of the room.

"What now?"

"Your place is closer than mine."

"Okay ..."

The moaning had stopped; he didn't know if it was a good sign or not. The shock was stoppering the overwhelming thought that it was all his fault. For the time being, they had to move him to safety. Just as they got to the threshold, Marion appeared, along with two or three of the others.

"Peter! What the hell happened?"

"We found him like this – I think they were torturing him – his arm is broken. We have to get him to Toby's. Why are you here? What's going on?"

"We came to warn you; everyone was mustering but Marshal and Manager were looking for you. They were asking everyone. I told them you were at the farm."

"Shit; no time!"

"The fire was under control. What do we do, Peter?"

Didn't David always say he was the bossy one? He didn't think he was bossy, maybe a little too full of himself at times if he were completely honest. Hadn't he always just tried to make them – everyone - happy? He looked at the pale, worried faces, keenly feeling their need for someone – him – to make everything right, everything better.

Ronan groaned; he snapped his eyes to the man's face, which was cut, swollen, and bruised from repeated punches. He could only guess at the pain.

"Marion; can you and the others take Ronan to Toby's? Look after him until I get back."

"What are you going to do, Peter?"

"Finish this ..."

They very carefully handed Ronan to the girls; he saw Marion take the lead as he hoped she would. They'd all have to do things they weren't ready for.

"Toby; come with me ... We have to get to the cemetery."

They took a different route, keeping out of sight for the main part. It was a longer route but avoided the main areas. At one point, they ran along the edge of the new conduit and Peter realised that it was carrying the electricity cables for the lighting in the tunnel.

"How long have we been duped?"

"Peter?"

"Nothing; you've got to get the town, Toby – I don't trust anyone else to go."

"What do I do when I get there?"

"Avoid anyone who looks to be in charge; find someone who looks like one of the cleaners – give them the note. Try and find someone who knew Ali Ben ... I'd go myself, Toby-"

"It's okay; I know. What they did to Ronan wasn't right."

When they came to the open ground that separated the compound proper and the cemetery, they ran as if their lives depended on it. When they sank down behind the wall to catch their breath, Peter made Toby check the bag.

"It's gonna take a few hours to get there; maybe there's a road hidden the other side of the scrub – Ronan and I didn't have time to look for it. Take it steady."

"I got this; don't worry. Make them pay for Ronan."

Nothing else needed to be said. They manhandled the door open and slipped inside. They ran along the corridor; nothing appeared to have been moved. The outer door was open just as he and Ronan had left it.

"Thank god; I hope this means they don't know that we know about this. Please be careful, Toby."

"I will – now go."

They hugged before Toby slipped away, picking a path between the lethal thorn bushes. He turned and raised his hand before he disappeared out of sight.

oOo

He left the doors open; it was impossible to lift them by himself in any event. When he re-emerged behind the wall of the cemetery, he crouched down while he took stock. He had no idea how he was meant to mobilise a hundred people. What did *make them pay* actually mean?

He knew he couldn't convince everyone of the truth in time.

"I have to make *them* tell everyone ..."

Just as he was about to get up, he heard voices.

"Find them! If this gets out, we're gonna have a load more shit to deal with!"

He recognised the voice as belonging to one of the assistant Marshals.

He crawled along to the corner of the wall, the furthest from the path back to the compound, and ducked behind it. When he dared to peek out, he saw two or three of the Techs and the assistant Marshal moving towards the open doorway but for now, none of them realised it was open.

He daren't show himself so he crawled away from the corner.

When he heard the shout that told him that they had found the open door, he got up and ran as fast as he could, not daring to look back.

Instinctively, he went back through the dome village, thinking it would provide more hiding places. When he came to his own gate, he was tempted to stop if only to grab some water. He dithered.

"Stop right there, son!"

oOo

He'd only had dealings with Marshal once before. That occasion when he and David, aged ten, had played truant, as most kids did at one time. They'd sneaked into the pool area, holing up to eat crackers and convince each other they were braver than anyone else.

Apparently, everyone playing truant, headed for the pool to eat crackers and boast about their courage. It hadn't taken more than thirty minutes before Marshal found them, who walloped their backsides before dragging them back to class. It had hurt but the badge of honour earned from the escapade more than compensated for the hours of detention.

He spun on his heel to find the man standing fifty feet away. He, like Manager, Director, and most of the others, had never been in *cryo*. The lines etched into his face, around his eyes and the corners of his mouth suggested to him someone in their fifties. Knowing what he did of things now, he had to wonder where the man had come from – where any of them had come from.

"We're gonna take this nice and easy; you're going to come with me and-"

"I'm not going anywhere with you; I know what you did – what you've all been doing!"

"Manager wants to talk to you-"

"Like he talked to Ronan? I've seen what you did to him."

The man advanced; panic started to roil through his gut, but he knew he'd be dead meat if he allowed himself to be caught.

Barricading himself in the pod would only stall the inevitable.

"Manager just wants to talk; nothing-"

"I've seen the dead cleaners ..."

The man stalled, clearly not expecting the revelation. The atmosphere changed instantly, becoming heavy and cloying but also tinged with something sharp like the disinfectant when you got it in a cut.

He saw the man swallow hard, and knew it meant his time was up.

"Run!" He screamed in his head, knowing what he needed to do but a kind of hopelessness robbed him of the impetus as if his shoes were made of lead.

He dropped his head, in a way inviting the fatal blow. He espied the digging fork that he had thrown into the long grass.

Fleetingly, he felt Ali Ben's fingertips caressing his cheek. He'd never expected to find such tenderness beneath the feral exterior. Thinking about him, lying dead, in a sack, piled up with the others, denied a proper burial, denied justice, spurred him on. Only later would he recognise the terror but also the hatred that had given him the means.

In a split second, catching sight of the man begin to pick up his pace, narrowing the gap between them, he fell to his knees, rolled, grabbed the shaft of the digging fork and as he came out of the roll, he launched the tool at the man like he was throwing a javelin.

There was a moment when he thought he'd missed because the man kept coming, but then he stumbled, spewing up blood, and when he fell, he impaled himself and when he landed on the ground, the teeth of the fork were poking out of his back.

By rights, he should have collapsed in shock, but it opened a doorway to a place where he felt light, powerful, and clean, like an arrow flying through the air, quivering along its length but nonetheless singing as it split in two the very molecules of air that dared to impede its progress.

He grabbed the man's keys and security card and fled in the direction of Toby's pod.

oOo

He found the door barricaded. When he called out, Marion answered.

"I'm alone! Quickly!!"

He was admitted. He found Marion and the girls plus two of the other boys.

"How is he?"

"He's sleeping – what happened?"

He rattled off the bare facts. One of the guys stumbled to the bathroom to throw up. Marion ran to his side.

"Oh, Peter!"

He expected her to slump into his arms, but he detected a force like he'd never felt in her before, something unbending yet strangely maternal.

"We have to see this through ..."

"From what we know, everyone else is corralled in the mess hall. Benjamin and Mitch escaped and came here, looking for Toby."

"I have his keys and his security pass."

"Everyone has to know what happened – you're going to have to get into Manager's office and use the announcer – it's the only way. Take Benjamin and Mitch with you."

"What about Ronan?"

"He's sleeping; he's okay – go!"

He knew it was now or never. As soon as Marshal's body was discovered, all hell would break loose.

"Okay, let's go!"

The three men barrelled out, and with Benjamin and Mitch covering his flanks, they made for the office suite. They saw no one en route. The reason was clear when they arrived in the quadrangle. A group of Techs and the assistant Marshals were barring the door to the mess hall, keeping everyone inside, he assumed. They halted in front of the doors to the R&D laboratory just in time.

"In here!" he whispered. The outer door yielded, gaining them access to the foyer. Using the security pass, they gained access to the corridor behind the short front desk. It was deserted. They scooted to the very end, finding their way barred by another door.

"Where does this lead; do either of you know?"

"Into the Hive's sub-level ... I'm sure there's a way out into the offices ..."

Having to steel himself, half-fighting the idea that there was still a line to cross, his hand wavered over the card reader.

"Peter?"

He'd killed a man; there were no more lines to cross. He just hoped the ocean of horror would not rise up and drown him before it was over.

He swiped the card and the lock clicked.

oOo

In a future time, after so much had changed, he'd remember this moment – the appalling fascination and utter desolation he felt in his heart at the scene that unfolded as they navigated the huge machinery and the forest of cables and tubes.

When they happened across a lowly Tech, presumably forgotten by everyone else in the melee, siphoning off something from one of the tubes through a complex array of taps and valves, any line there might have been was quickly erased.

"Who are you?" and the man's voice betrayed all his worst fears.

"What are you doing?"

The man started to back away, but Benjamin and Mitch moved quickly to cut off his retreat.

"What are you doing!"

"I ... I'm harvesting plasma-"

"What do you mean *harvesting plasma* – from them?" and Peter glanced up and saw the full scale of the terrifying truth.

"Y-yes – you shouldn't be here! You have to go!"

"What else do you harvest?"

"B-blood products, bone marrow, stem cells, spinal fluid-"

"You fucking monster!" and before Benjamin and Mitch could stop him, he had his hands around the man's throat. "You fucking monster!" It took a minute before he regained any self-control and released his grip, ordering Benjamin to find something with which to tie the man's hands, adding, "You're coming with us."

As they passed through the rest of the facility, he saw the same boxes he had seen piled up in the tunnel.

"Where is it being sent?"

"E-everywhere – we export it everywhere ..."

Only then did the terrifying reality come into sharp focus – they weren't survivors of the holocaust; they were being farmed like a crop and milked like a herd.

"Upstairs ..."

Forcing the man to guide them through the labyrinth of passageways and stairways, they arrived at the back of the office suite, into what looked like the private dining room.

Benjamin and Mitch held the man while Peter tripped over to the door that led out into a yet another foyer, but one he recognised as the reception area in front of Manager's office. Through the narrow, glazed aperture, he could see the office – the door was partly ajar – and it appeared empty. We waved the others over.

"Once we're in the office, you two guard the door – you and I have an announcement to make ..." he didn't recognise his voice. It sounded like what he imagined the soldier's voice sounded like – the blond one, wearing the medallion, dropping down behind the bunker, level up his gun to wreak destruction.

He turned to the Tech, "If you don't do exactly what I say, I'll kill you just like the Marshal and I swear to god, I'll fucking bleed you of every fluid in your body – do you understand?!"

He nodded. The whiff of piss alerted them to the fact that he'd wet himself.

"Go!"

oOo

He recognised the opulence for exactly what it was now – the desk and the rest of the furniture were not *plasto* like everywhere else. There were plants in pots on shelves that he hadn't notice before.

He sat down at the desk, suddenly aware of the fact that his trainers were sinking into the thick pile of the rug beneath his feet. Eyeing the man, seated in the chair on the opposite side of the desk, he picked up the announcer and clicked the red button on the side of the hand-held device.

"This is Peter ..."

He released the button and palmed his face, conscious of the fact that his lips were dry, and his tongue was sticking to the roof of his mouth. He reached for the water, lifting the jug to his lips.

He started again.

"This is Peter ... Everything we have ever been told is a lie – a dirty lie ... First, if Manager is listening, know this ... I have seen the harvesters beneath the Hive, and I have a Tech here who will tell everyone one what you're really doing-"

A crash from outside announced the arrival of the assistant Marshals and the Techs who had been guarding the mess hall. They piled into the foyer and rushed the door.

Peter turned to the Tech, "Will the door hold?"

"This is the most secure room in the compound; no one is getting in ..."

"What's your name?"

"Stephen ..."

"Okay; you know what to say ..."

Peter turned the microphone back on, "... Listen to what Stephen has to say – no one should feel afraid, no one need do what they tell you – this is over ..."

He handed the microphone to Stephen, "Tell the truth ... You owe Marion's baby that much ..."

He watched as the man readied himself, no doubt weighing his options, agreeing with himself in the end that he had no choice, and more than that, he could no longer live with the knowledge that he'd accumulated over years of service.

"My name is Stephen; I'm a Tech in the Hive ..."

Chapter Eight – Noble Scholar

"Status, Marion?"

"Eighteen dead ..."

He thought he'd never regret the carnage after Stephen's announcement when Manager and the rest had been ripped to pieces in the quadrangle as if they had been set upon by a pack of wild dogs.

He hadn't banked on one of the Techs sabotaging the Hive.

He sat back, not in Manager's chair in Manager's office, but in a makeshift command post in the mess hall, being the most central place where anyone could come and see him, sometimes to report, as Marion had, more often, to talk.

"... I've informed the partners ... Marie said all the children were okay ... Peter?"

"Eighteen ... I-"

"No; not your fault."

"I was going to say that maybe I should have told the partners – thank you ... How are Gwen and David?"

"Recovering well ... Everyone has been told something – not too much; we don't want to cause them any more trauma than necessary ... You look tired; get something to eat and grab a few hours' sleep ..."

"How's Ronan?"

"Healing ... His arm has been set and splinted – he'll be okay. We need to decide what to do with the bodies ..."

He wasn't sure if she meant the eighteen or Manager and the rest.

"Proper burials for our friends ..."

It was no good; he couldn't hold it back any longer and he broke down in a quake of sobs. Marion rushed to his side and put her arms around him, cradling his cheek against her breast.

"Shush ... It's over ... Proper burials for our friends ... The rest are being burned – no trace left behind – agreed?"

"A-agreed ..."

He gathered himself together and wiped his eyes, suffering Marion to frame his face in her hands and kiss his forehead.

"I'll check on the kids and then grab something to eat – what about you?"

"Don't worry about me; us girls have everything under control. Thank you …"

He wasn't sure what she was thanking him for.

"Thank you?"

"You alone – no; you and Ronan, to be accurate – did what I don't think anyone else could have done … We're free, Peter – whatever happens now, we're free to make the decisions for ourselves."

"I just hope Toby is alright …"

"We'll have to wait and see. The doors to the outside have been secured just in case. One of the boys is posted as look-out-"

"We must bury all the cleaners too – and-"

"Just relax; it will be done – if you want to do anything, think about how we go forward. Everyone is in shock – more or less. Pretty soon, everyone is going to ask the same question …"

"What do you want, Marion?"

She took a moment to answer.

"I want peace … I want everyone to be together … and I want a baby …"

He might have guessed it, but it still took him by surprise.

"After everything?"

"*Especially* after everything … A baby born in our new world, who'll never know separation from its mother and never know separation from the person they love …"

After that, she drifted away, and he felt more at peace himself. Despite the crushing tiredness, he got up and walked out. There were still people about, some young teens, not really sure what they should be doing, and a few of the older teens, trying to get everyone into bed.

"I'll put the film on; what do you say?"

"Really?"

"Yeah; I expect there's ice cream somewhere too – come on ..."

Yes, he'd seen it a hundred and one times but the story of the children lost in the forest never seemed more apt than at that precise moment. By the time he had the film running, practically all the seats were taken. He found a spare seat next to one of the young teens.

"I'm Billy – you're Peter."

"Yes, I am - pleased to know you, Billy."

"You saved us, didn't you?"

"Yeah, I suppose I did – with help from Ronan and Toby – and a few others."

"Marie says that we won't have to go in the Hive now – is that true?"

"Yes, it's true – no one will ever have to go into the Hive ever again."

"Thank you ..."

He let the tears roll down his face unabashed. When the children walked out of the forest and found the windmill, he screamed louder than any of the rest.

oOo

"Is it true?"

"Lookout reports smoke rising from the town – about half an hour ago ..."

"Keep me posted ..."

He called on Marion in the kitchen, who was just completing the inventory of their supplies and looking pretty happy.

"So much food, Peter. I know we have more mouths to feed but we have enough – and the idea to turn the Hive into a vertical farm and grow more fresh stuff is sheer genius – what's wrong?"

"Lookout reports smoke rising from the town – what do we do? Do we send a party out?"

"It's been four days ..."

"Who can we spare?"

"Benjamin and Mitch – Ronan wants to see you by the way ..."
"Should we go out?"
"We can't ignore it, Peter. Something has obviously happened – it might be good for us. Talk to Ronan. We can spare two boys ... And David and Gwen are out of high care ..."

He'd been dreading it if he were honest.

He found Ronan, who was supervising the clean-up of the library.

"Ronan!"
"Peter!"
"I hope you're not overdoing it."
"Just doing a little ... I heard David and Gwen were out of high care ..."
"Yes; they are. Marion just told me. Before that, we have to decide if we send a party to the town. Smoke has been seen rising ... What did you want to see me about?"

If a look could communicate an ocean of feelings and questions, Ronan's managed it.

"I suppose it all boils down to who you want to be with ..."

And never had so much been put into a nutshell quite so succinctly.

"I need to talk to Gwen, Ronan ... and David ..."

He knew he was being naïve if those few words alone were enough to communicate the true nature of how things actually stood.

Ronan eyed him quizzically, knowing there was more to it than he appreciated.

"... Just give me a little time. First things first; do we send out a party?"

"We have to know what's happening and we can't abandon Toby ..."
"I know. Benjamin and Mitch are free – I should go too."

The intersections of all the emotions looked like the shards of the broken glass that were being swept up. He wondered if things would ever fit back together right.

"You're needed here; I'll go with them – I'm next to useless while I can't use my arm."

"It could be dangerous."

"No more dangerous than being locked up and punched in the face a hundred times ... I was the one who saw the wind turbine first – it feels right that I should go too ..."

Was this leadership? Weighing up the odds of success and failure, sacrificing an individual's needs for the greater good – was that how it all began; did it, therefore, follow that it would also end in the same way?

"You need to rest and finish healing; I'll go ..."

Leaders led their people; wasn't that how it was done, he asked himself.

Ronan said nothing more and returned to the task of clearing up.

He walked out and headed for the clinic.

oOo

"Stephen!"

"Hello, Peter! How are things?"

"Busy! How are our patients?"

"All doing well ... I have to thank you for letting me do this ... after, you know, what you saw – after what happened."

"You're valuable, Stephen – you alone know how most of these machines work. If you're asking me if I trust you, I think you have little left to prove. You are different from the rest of them. They came from the city; you didn't."

Stephen alone knew how things had been managed. There were towns and cities all over the region. Most were small and developing, eking out an existence just like them. The largest of the cities had provided the key staff and the technology years and years before. Stephen had been born in the compound; both his parents had been Tech. He knew no other life.

Peter had already asked the question - Why had they recruited the cleaners from the town?

Stephen didn't know; he had rarely left the basement under the Hive.

"I need to see Gwen and David – are they awake?"

"Yes ... Just five minutes though today, okay?"

"Okay ..."

He wandered into the ward, speaking to everyone, reassuring those who needed it, answering questions, and promising to do whatever he was asked to do. Those who had been in high care were transferred to a sideward for a few days to be monitored and assessed before being moved to the general ward, ultimately being released back into the community. Gwen and David alone were in the sideward. Two others were still in intensive care.

He was greeted by one of the trainee nurses.

"Hello, Peter."

"Hello, Danni ... How are they doing?"

"Gwen is fine; just another forty-eight hours rest, and she can move to low dependency ... David is having difficulty remembering things – consequence of the brain being starved of oxygen. Because he was the furthest away, he was reached last ..."

"Thank you ..."

He stepped through the doors and immediately found Gwen, sitting upright, reading.

"Peter!"

"Gwen ..."

He stepped up and wrapped her in his arms, never more grateful to whoever had answered his prayers.

"I'm so pleased to see you! You look like shit, but I guess you know that already ... Maybe you should be resting here for a couple of days!"

"I'm fine; I'm just so happy and relieved that you're okay ... Is there anything I can do for you? Is there anything you want to know?"

She leaned back to look him straight in the eye.

"What?"

"You're lost to me, aren't you? You're going to be paired with this now ..." and she raised her hand and gestured out of the window.

"I don't know what you mean-"

"You're going to be everyone's father and brother now – I can see it in your eyes and in your voice – I see it and hear it in theirs. Don't get me wrong; I don't think anyone else could do what needs to be done ... It's okay; I think the fact that we never managed to have a baby should probably tell us that it was time for us to part-"

"But ... I've only just got you back."

"You haven't lost me, Peter; you *have* gained a better friend than you can imagine ..."

He was dumbfounded. It was the last thing he had expected to hear.

"I still love you, Gwen ..."

"And I still love you ... Be warned; he's changed-"

"Who?"

"David ... He doesn't remember much – he vaguely recognises me – just go easy; don't get upset ..."

He moved down the ward to the opposite side of the room, to the last bed, by the window. David appeared to be asleep. He drew up a chair and sat down by the side of the bed, and just gazed at the face of his lifelong friend and lover of more than ten years.

"David; can you hear me?"

David's eyes flickered and then opened. Turning his head and smiling, he said, "Hello ..."

"Hello, David. How are you feeling?"

"Not too bad – someone said there might be ice cream today; do you know if they were telling the truth?"

"You can have ice cream every day, David ..."

"Every day?"

"Yes ... Do you recognise me, David?"

"I ... I don't think so - vaguely. You know my name, but I don't know yours ..."

Only then did he understand the true cost of the choices he had made – sacrificing the needs of the individual for the greater good? Only then did he realise that it had been his needs that had been sacrificed.

"My name is *Peter* ..."

There was no glimmer of recognition, just the same dimpled smile that he had known his entire life.

"*Peter* ... It is a nice name ... Do you know what film we're having tonight?"

"Which film would you like?"

"I can choose?!"

"Of course!"

"What about the one about the shipwreck – I love that one."

"Okay ... Why don't you rest for a bit and later, I'll come by and we can go and watch the film together?"

"I'd like that ..."

He quit David's bedside and sought out the nurse, asking the obvious question.

"He may regain something of his memories but, to be honest, I wouldn't hold out much hope ..."

He went to find Marion.

"No recognition ... Gwen is fine. Tomorrow, Benjamin, Mitch and I will go to the town; can you prep some food for us?"

"Sure ... I hate to give you another job to do but accommodation needs to be sorted now that everyone is out. We have teens who need a place to live and some of those who lost someone want to double up rather be on their own ..."

"I'll draw up a plan for us to discuss – what about you and David?"

"He'll need support for a while – I'll take care of him. What about you and Gwen?"

"I need to find somewhere else – somewhere out of the way if I plan to get *any* sleep."

"There's the pod behind the botanical garden – the last one to be built. It's empty."

"Thank you ..."

He trooped back to the dome and packed his meagre possessions, transferring them to the pod by the greenhouse. It had the benefit of being out of the main compound.

He unpacked; it was a task of fifteen minutes. A knock at the door interrupted his train of thought.

"Coming!"

It was Ronan.

"Can I come in?"

"Of course ..."

He stepped back, already craving contact, but holding himself in check.

When he turned around after the closing the door, he found Ronan getting undressed.

"Ronan-"

"Shush ... I know it's going to be difficult at first – and you're going tomorrow ... Just lie down with me and hold me ..."

He hadn't even made the bed.

"What about Amy?"

"We'd already made the decision ... Just lie down ..."

Carefully, avoiding his splinted arm, he lay down and gathered Ronan up in his arms as best he could.

"Nothing will need to be said. Everyone will figure it out on their own, Peter."

He didn't know if he had the same faith.

"I can't believe no one will have a problem – it's human nature."

"Then on top of everything else, it's up to us to show them that it's perfectly normal and nothing to be ashamed of ... Now be quiet and just hold me ..."

oOo

Marion and Ronan accompanied them to the outer hatch cover.

"Once we close the cover, lock it, okay? Take no chances. We'll be back as soon as we can. Take care, Marion. Don't overdo it, Ronan."

"Take care ..."

Ronan said nothing and just smiled.

Once they had climbed the steps and out into the thorn bush-dotted scrubland, they closed the door and waited to hear the locking bars slide into place.

"Let's go!"

Just as Toby had found for himself, beyond the scrubland, first angling north, and then turning west, there was a trackway. Initially, it was nothing more than two faint, shallow grooves in the dirt created by – they had no clue but guessed a vehicle.

It made the going easy for a time. When they dropped beneath the edge of the rough plateau, it got decidedly more humid. In a series of switchbacks, they descended to the floor of what they recognised as a broad valley. Already details were easier to pick out – the individual blades of the turbines ... and the unmistakable column of black smoke rising from the town, which was still too far away to make out anything specifically except for a whiteish, fuzzy blob.

"Domes?" queried Mitch.

"Would make sense – supplied by the city like the rest," Peter suggested.

"As long as it's just the domes that are the same ..."

He didn't want to think about the possibility of another Hive community.

Once they were on the valley floor, their path looked to be laid out; there was a more distinct trackway leading off into the distance in the direction of the town. In places, it forded small streams, and in others, the track was carried over wider watercourses by simple bridges made of what looked like *plastocrete*.

At midday, they stopped and had something to eat, feasting on the food that Marion had found in the private kitchen that had fed the elite. He was a little embarrassed but also encouraged by what Marion had said as she'd handed over the supplies.

"I'm not wasting it, Peter – everyone is having some before it spoils, and we're harvesting any seeds we can find for the new farm ..."

It seemed like a good time to discuss the future.

"We are going to have a new farm, and more freedom – but else do we want?"

Mitch was the one to voice his fears.

"Some may wish to leave – others may wish to join us – keeping the doors locked is not an option now, but are we ready for that?"

"Not yet, but we have to expect it. I suppose what we find here may tell us how ready we will need to be ..."

He hadn't voiced one particular fear, and he hoped no one else did for the time being, but if they opened their doors, would they also need to arm themselves?

Benjamin was more succinct.

"We need to decide as a community what we want and what we don't ..."

They bathed in one of the clear, fast-running streams. It felt so good to wash away the dust and the sweat. The dried off quickly in the early afternoon heat. The valley floor was devoid of trees and there was little shade. The turbines became clearer and clearer with every step, but the town was lost in the heat haze.

"Perhaps it is no bad thing that they won't see our approach," Peter offered.

"How do we approach, Peter – assuming this track leads up to the front door ..."

"I have a feeling we are going to know when we get a bit closer – there's more smoke ..."

They trudged on until the late afternoon when it was clear they would not reach the town before dark. They rested.

"Do we go on, Peter?"

"Under the cover of darkness? We have torches ... Rest first and start again in the early hours?"

"Yeah – get there around dawn ..."

They carried on until they came across a watercourse with a bridge.

"Camp here? It's flat, smooth and dry."

"Good call ..."

They had no tents or bedding, just a blanket apiece. It wasn't cold at all but after the sun went down, they could sense a fresher air coming in from the south.

"From the ocean?"

"That's what it looked like to me and Ronan from up there – just nothing but water. There was a river flowing out from the base of the bluff. It would be nice to explore this land, wouldn't it?"

"It's weird to think that pretty much no one in the community is older than twenty-six ... just think how far you could get before you were too old ..."

Sitting with his knees drawn up to his chest and his blanket draped around his shoulders, Peter contemplated the darkening sky and the emerging stars. It was hours before the moon rose. Seated there, he imagined how it would feel to float through Space – it was a tantalizing prospect, but he somehow knew he would always be happy in the community.

oOo

As the moon rose, Peter led them out single file. Each had a torch, but it was bright enough to see without them.

After a couple of hours, the dry, dusty, stony trail stopped abruptly. They switched on their torches to investigate. The trail ahead appeared to disappear in just nothingness. Upon closer inspection, the track had given way to a broad, black, solid road, more like the paths in the compound, which were made from compacted stone and dressed in the finer sand. The surface of the road was hard, made from small stones mixed with a dark compound.

"We must be getting nearer ..."

Progress was swift, and for a time they jogged, taking advantage of the cooler air. Soon the torches were superfluous, and they bagged them, grabbing food and water at the same time.

"Can you hear that?" Benjamin asked.

They strained their ears and picked up on a low-level, deep, thrumming.

"A generator?"

"The turbines?"

"We're definitely getting close ..."

They jogged more slowly, keeping their eyes peeled for more signs. The next bridge, which was the longest and broadest that they had encountered so far gave them the first clue.

"What does it say?" asked Mitch.

"... *M-b-a-t-h-w-i* ..."

"It's the name of the town – that's what Ali Ben said ..."

The sign beside the bridge looked old but cared for. A little further, the road was crossed by another, each arm disappearing into the distance. The next clue to their whereabouts was more sobering; the air tasted acrid and smelled of burning *plasto*.

"It can't be much further ..."

And Peter was right. Sure enough, less than an hour later, just as dawn was about to break, they reached a steep hill, steep enough that they were panting by the time they reached the top. When they stepped over the brow, the scene before them was not that much different to the chaos they had only just escaped. The town beneath them, which stretched nearly as far as the foothills, was enclosed in a shallow depression. The hill they had just climbed appeared to encircle it. Fires were burning in many places. Isolated shrieks cut through the air.

"What are we going to do, Peter?"

He was scanning, looking for a better way in – wondering where the hell they were going to find Toby.

Within the bowl, the town itself appeared to be encircled by a wall but one that was much lower than the one that enclosed their own. It seemed to be pierced at regular intervals by openings, possibly large gates.

"Let's go slow; there must be a main entrance ..."

They followed the road, dropping down all the while. Then it was clear that the road circumnavigated the city, and like the spokes of a wheel, roads led off from the encircling track and disappeared inside the city through the gates, many of which were barred.

They circled north to find an open gate. It also brought them closer to the forest of turbines – the source of the deep thrumming.

Louder and more distinct sounds were filtering out now. The air was becoming thicker with smoke.

As they moved around the circle, they passed out of the smoke, and their view of the wall and the gates cleared. Finally, they saw something that looked like the main entrance into the city. The gate was bigger and more ornately decorated – which they found strange as nothing in the Hive complex was decorated at all. And crucially, the gate was open. Even at their distance – still five hundred metres – they could make out two or three men, standing in a knot outside.

"Do we approach, Peter?"

"I don't think we have a choice ... I'll go first; stay behind me. Any sign of trouble, just run back to the Hive – okay?"

"Okay ..."

They marched with purpose. Their approach went unnoticed until they were within hailing distance. A shout went up and one of the men disappeared through the gate into the city. The other two men started to walk out.

"Easy ... I'll introduce us ..."

When they were no more than twenty metres apart, Peter and the boys stopped, as did the men.

"My name is Peter; this is Benjamin and Mitch – we've come from the compound. We're looking for Toby ..."

He wondered if the men had understood anything he had said.

The larger of the two men, who stood a head above the other, struck a remarkable resemblance to Marshal. The other man, shorter and slimmer, with blond hair, smiled and stepped forward a few paces.

"Welcome ... My name is Yves, and this is Daniel. The other man you saw was Gregory. We have been waiting for you."

"Is Toby here?"

"He is injured – not seriously, I hasten to add. If you would like to follow me, I'll take you to him. You'll forgive our poor hospitality – there's been some trouble, as you can see."

"What happened?"

"I think I would describe it as an uprising – Toby would be the better one to ask – he started it. Come; you don't have to fear us ..."

Taking the first step forward was perhaps the most difficult thing he had ever done. He sensed Benjamin and Mitch at his shoulders. He breathed deeply and straightened his shirt.

As he moved forward, he asked, "Did you know the man called *Ali Ben?*"

"Most people have heard of *Ali Ben* – we know what happened; Toby told us. If he hadn't had the medallion, things may have gone very differently ..."

They moved forward. When they were but two metres away, Yves thrust out his hand.

"Welcome to *Noble City*-"

"*Noble?*"

"That's right - *Noble City* ..."
"What is the meaning of *Noble Scholar?*"
"The name of the founder of our city was a man called *Noble Scholar-*"
"The name on the back of-"
"the medallion – yes. He was a soldier in The Wars-"
"You look just like him – we have a film, he's the soldier ..."
"I am related ... Come ..."

Peter reached out and shook the man's hand. The man's grip was firm and heartfelt, he sensed, almost as if their arrival had been eagerly awaited.

"How did Toby get hurt?"

"I suspect he may tell a *slightly* different story – he stepped in the way of a bullet and it grazed his arm – a flesh wound, no more. That is not to say he was not brave because he was, especially when so few would join him at the start, fearing reprisals ... Had he not found someone who knew *Ali Ben* when he first entered the city, things probably would not have gone so well. He tells me there has been trouble – I assume from your appearance today that the elite have been-"

"Overthrown ... Yes, there has been trouble; many of our friends were killed ..."

It was hard to concentrate. As they moved through the portal, the city in all its glory was revealed to them. The whiteish blob they had seen from the top of the scarp was not a collection of domes as they had predicted, but a glittering collection of majestic buildings fronting broad avenues, radiating out like the spokes of a wheel from a hub that was dominated by a large square, a fountain, and a building the like of which Peter and the boys had never seen.

"What is that place, Yves?"

"The cathedral – a place of worship – where we pray to our god ..."

"What are the buildings made of?"

"White granite with a high concentration of mica – the mica gives it the sparkle – you won't find much *plastocrete* here ..."

"It's breath-taking ..."

"Come along; Gregory will have announced your arrival; I'm sure Toby will be very keen, and no doubt relieved to see you ..."

Yves and Daniel – who said practically nothing – led them through one quarter to a huge complex of the white buildings.

"The hospital ..."

"Wow ... We have a clinic – hospital beds for about twenty. This is monumental. How many people live here?"

"Thirty thousand-"

"Thirty thousand?!"

"We are small compared to other cities ..."

After what seemed like an age, wandering along endless corridors, past ward after ward of pristine white beds, though as they progressed, many more of the beds were occupied, they arrived at a quieter area.

"Toby is in here. It was better for everyone – he has assumed hero status ..."

Peter turned to Mitch and Benjamin and just shook his head.

Yves pushed open a door into a suite of single rooms. At the end of a short corridor, they found Gregory beside an open door.

"Gregory; this is Peter and Mitch and Benjamin – they are here to see Toby. Is he fit to receive visitors?"

"The nurse is just changing the dressing on his wound."

They waited patiently for the nurse to emerge.

"Don't overtax him; he needs to rest!"

"Yes, ma'am ..."

Yves turned to the boys, "Go on; afterwards, we'll get something to eat and you can meet everyone ..."

Peter stepped through the door.

"What took you so long?"

"Hello, Toby ... Hero, huh?"

"I don't like to brag-"
"Since when?"

Chapter Ten – Unification

"We have to get back, Toby – are you sure you won't come back with us?"

"I want to stay and learn as much as possible – I'll be back soon, I promise."

"Okay ... Do you have the letter for Denise?"

"It's here. Please ask her to think hard about joining me. For fuck's sake, just hug me!"

The last forty-eight hours had been the most difficult and yet the most amazing in their lives.

"Don't do anything more than *averagely* heroic."

"You're just jealous – I won't. Boy; we are on the cusp of something truly amazing, Peter."

"I hope you're right, but I think we need to take it slow."

"If Yves and the Council's invitation is taken up by the majority, you may have to think about abandoning the compound – and why would you stay there when you can have all this?"

"It'll be up to each and every one of us to make his or her own decision – we'll see you soon. Take care."

"Take care, dude ..."

He joined the others in the courtyard of the building where Toby had been moved after his release from the hospital. Benjamin and Mitch together with Yves were loading the supplies into the back of the motorised carryall for the journey home.

"Is he staying, Peter?"

"Yes; nothing will convince him to leave here ... Are you still planning to come with us, Yves?"

"Yes; just for a few days – I want to meet everyone, and we need to establish communication links and work out some of the finer details of the offer – don't worry; we don't plan to take over ... In any event, we have a lot of work to do here first ... Repatriation of the bodies is the first priority ... Are we set, boys?"

"We're good!"

With medical supplies, comms equipment, seeds, books, films, foodstuffs, and the al- important letters – the one from Toby to Denise, and the one from the Council – they headed out and quickly passed under the arch of the main gate. Within minutes, the city was already receding into the heat haze.

"What will happen to the old Council members, Yves?"

"There is talk of a trial, but I have my doubts that it will help – I have to say, I would rather most people did not know the extent of their crimes; I think the wounds are deep enough and will take at least a generation to properly heal ... They'll plead ignorance of the facts, blaming Guardian for keeping them in the dark – we know they were fully briefed but when Toby and the insurgents stormed the council hall, many documents that would have proved their undeniable guilt, were destroyed – I'm hoping you have documents we can use to make the case stick."

"And integration of the *Mbathwian?*"

"Stands a much better chance now after what Toby did – we all share in that shame; most of us did not want to know the truth. Confronting that will be just as hard. Repatriating the bodies will be the beginning ..."

They drove on in companionable silence. Very quickly, they arrived at the trailhead where the made road ran out. They switched to caterpillar tracks. Peter and others were amazed at the quality of the technology – living a life surrounded by such machines and tools was very alluring but there was a reality too – the need to have jobs, earn credits, pay for food and accommodation – it was as bewildering as it was scary.

"I have to get back by noon tomorrow, Peter but once we can communicate with one another, things will be so much easier. I would caution against making too many changes at once – start a dialogue ..."

These ideas felt altogether too adult – how easy had life been when every decision had been someone else's to make – the only effort, to reconcile personal needs with the needs of the Hive, which had never felt *that* hard, but maybe that was a function of believing there was nothing else, no choice, and no expectation of it ever being different.

Having set a lookout, it came as no surprise when, as they arrived at the entrance to the tunnel, there was a welcoming committee of sorts. Two faces stood out in the sea of faces – Ronan's and Marion's.

Peter stepped forward to reassure everyone that everything was fine. Almost immediately, he was swamped by the youngsters.

"Everything is fine – come and meet Yves ..."

Once he had extricated himself, leaving Yves to introduce himself and show the older children around the carryall, he met up with Ronan and Marion.

They hugged very warmly.

"Hey, you guys."

"Hello, Peter – where's Toby?"

"Where to begin? There's a lot to tell you – Toby is fine; he's staying in the city for now. We need to unload the supplies and get everyone together to introduce Yves properly. I have to speak to Denise as soon as possible. Has everyone been okay?"

"Everyone is fine ... Let's get everyone back inside ..."

He corralled the stragglers and made sure the supplies were all unloaded, locking the hatch himself, wondering how long it would be before they locked it for the last time.

oOo

"We're all set; don't hesitate to contact me, Peter. I think we both have our work cut out for the time being. Don't make any quick decisions; you may not appreciate it but your life here is much simpler than it would be in Noble. Take care, my friend ..."

"Thank you, Yves; thank you for everything – send Toby back if he starts to be a major pain in the arse!"

"I will. Kinda surprised that Denise didn't want to join him, but I think he'll understand that she's needed here more for now. Goodbye."

"Goodbye ..."

Their meeting, outside the hatch, was private. He hadn't felt the weight of his responsibilities as keenly than at this precise moment – and the threatened pace of change was becoming an overwhelming dread.

He watched as Yves drove away and didn't turn around until he was out of sight. When he turned, he found Ronan waiting for him.

"Hey; what's wrong?"

"Nothing – everything is fine. I just wanted you to myself ..."

And that was something else he never seemed to have – a minute to himself.

"Maybe we should open the pool and disappear to the dome while everyone is enjoying themselves ..."

He felt a rebel for suggesting it, but he was beginning to recognise the pain in his chest as the need to have Ronan in his arms.

"No objections from me; c'mon ..."

They locked up and wandered back through the compound, giving the order to open the pool, which had the desired outcome. They headed to the dome and closed the door, remembering to lock it, and only then did they relax.

"This will need to change, Peter – we need to start to be open about things ..."

"Yes; I know ... I have an idea that Gwen suspects; you need to have a conversation with Amy ..."

"Agreed, and then we say to hell with it as far as anyone else is concerned – yes?"

"Okay ... For now, can we just forget all about them?"

No answer was forthcoming as Ronan shed his clothes, getting himself tangled in his sling.

"Come here ... Can't wait for this to come off ..."

Ronan just smiled back at him, licking his lips. When Peter knelt down to ease him out of his shorts, he could not help himself and he kissed the object of his desire, nuzzling in between the swelling rod and the furry, tightening sack, breathing in the delicious scent of wet earth and dry stone, already letting go of his hold on his need, feeling the weight slip from his shoulders as he teased the ripening fruit of Ronan's cock with the tip of his tongue before sucking the pulsing head into his mouth, closing his eyes as Ronan gripped the back of his neck, pulling in, already tilting his pelvis.

oOo

"Do *you* want to go?" Ronan asked as they cooled off, side by side, after yet another sweaty session. It was late, well past midnight.

"I don't know ... It sounds strange to admit it, but I actually think I will be happier to stay here – but there is a reality – what about you?"

"I suppose it depends on how many want to go and how many choose to stay – I would like to visit the city and see it for myself."

"Everyone should – The hardest will be the children; they need their schooling ... I suspect we will not appreciate what we have lost until it is too late."

"But we cannot lock the doors and forget what we know ... It becomes its own kind of torment."

"Fuck me again and ask me then – torment is not having you inside me ..."

While Ronan was encumbered by the splint and sling, it was easier for Peter to squat over him and lower himself onto the proud rod that found its mark so readily. A combination of powerful upward thrusts and a steady rocking brought them both off together. Peter wasted no time in licking up the salty pearls and then kissing Ronan deeply to share his seed, finding this compulsion to impregnate each other more urgent and more vital than other feelings.

Intoxicated on the reek of sweat and sex, they finally crashed, sated, for the time being, knowing their need would never be fully satisfied.

"I love you, Ronan ..."

"I love you too ... As long as we're together, I don't care what else happens ..."

oOo

"Have you tallied the numbers, Marion? How many want to leave?"

After a period during which everyone visited the city for a few days, and a number of the Noble City residents had made the trip to the commune, largely to help establish the new farm with gifts of tools and plants, it was agreed that anyone who wished to go, would be free to leave, and if the number who wished to remain fell too low, the entire community would leave and resettle in Noble.

"I have just finished the count, which both Ronan and Denise have audited. I think you are going to be-"

"Disappointed?"

"I really didn't expect you to want to stay here – I don't know why. Disappointed? We agreed that if the commune were to remain viable, then at least thirty of us would have to remain ..."

"How many want to stay, Marion?"

He had made his feelings clear. He did want to stay. He and Ronan had visited the city and they had been welcomed with open arms ... but he had never felt so tiny and insignificant.

"Everyone wants to ..."

He was dreading the outcome. He knew relocating would be the right thing to do, but he also knew that he would never feel as free.

"... stay here."

"E-excuse me? Say that again ..."

"Everyone wants to stay here, Peter – only Toby wants to remain in Noble ..."

"I ... I don't believe it – why?"

"Because everyone knows that you want to stay here, and they would rather stay here with you than move and lose what we all treasure the most – our community and you leading us ..."

"But ... but after everything that has happened – the friends we've lost – all the years of toiling away for nothing ..."

"Yes, we have lost friends – and we won't forget them ... Then, we had no choice, now, we do, and if we choose to stay, we will be stronger than we've ever been, and above all, free ..."

He couldn't come to terms with it.

Just at that moment, a group of the younger children came running through on their way to the pool to have a swimming lesson. Their excited screams and shouts only died down when Marie promised them a treat. As the group disappeared, a couple, Thomas and Bridgette, came over to show him a tray of seedlings.

"Look, Peter; we've finally got the onions started!"

"Wow, guys; fantastic. What about the avocados?"

"Nothing yet ..."

"Okay. I'll be along soon to show you how to graft those new fruiting cherry scions onto the rootstock ..."

Wherever he looked, he could see someone doing something, smiling if not laughing.

He turned to Marion.

"... You truly believe we can do this?"

"We *are* doing this ..."

Epilogue

"Are we doing this?"

"Peter; we're going to breakfast like we do every day ..."

"Yeah ... but we're going together – hand-in-hand ..."

"You're worrying about nothing ... Let's go!"

It felt right; after six months, several conversations with both Amy and Gwen, it was time to let the world know how things stood.

"And you think there are others just waiting for this ... what are we calling it?"

"Sign ... I know there are others, Peter; everyone looks to you – whether you like it or not – it's up to you – and in this, us – to show everyone that it's *absolutely* normal and okay to love whoever you want."

"But we were never taught it was wrong."

"No, we weren't, but no one said it was right either – ever noticed how someone always has to dive into the pool first before anyone else will?"

www.ingramcontent.com/pod-product-compliance
Ingram Content Group UK Ltd.
Pitfield, Milton Keynes, MK11 3LW, UK
UKHW040901240225
455493UK00001B/131